Hubert Mingarelli is a French writer of numerous novels, short story collections, and fiction for young adults, and the winner of the *Prix Médicis* for his book *Quatre soldats*. He lives in Grenoble.

A MEAL IN WINTER

One morning in the dead of winter, three German soldiers are dispatched into the frozen Polish countryside to track down any Jews they can find — and return them for execution. Having captured a young man hiding in the woods, they rest in an abandoned house before continuing back to camp. But before long, the group's sympathies have splintered as they consider the moral implications of their mission, and confront their own consciences. Should the Jew be offered food? But after breaking bread with a man, how can they possibly send him to his death? Or should they risk everything to return him to liberty?

HUBERT MINGARELLI

A MEAL
IN WINTER

Translated from the French
by Sam Taylor

Complete and Unabridged

ULVERSCROFT
Leicester

First published in Great Britain in 2013 by
Portobello Books
London

First Large Print Edition
published 2017
by arrangement with
Portobello Books
London

A catalogue record for this book is available
from the British Library.

ISBN 978–1–4448–3373–7

Published by
F. A. Thorpe (Publishing)
Anstey, Leicestershire

Set by Words & Graphics Ltd.
Anstey, Leicestershire
Printed and bound in Great Britain by
T. J. International Ltd., Padstow, Cornwall

This book is printed on acid-free paper

They had rung the iron gong outside and it was still echoing, at first for real in the courtyard, and then, for a longer time, inside our heads. We would not hear it again. We had to get up straight away. Lieutenant Graaf never had to ring the iron twice. A meagre light came through the frost-covered window. Emmerich was sleeping on his side. Bauer woke him. It was late afternoon, but Emmerich thought it was morning. He sat up on his bed and looked at his boots, seeming not to understand why he'd slept in them all night.

In the meantime, Bauer and I had already put our boots on. Emmerich got up and went to look through the window, but he couldn't see anything because of the frost, so he kept on struggling to disentangle night from day. Bauer explained to him that it was afternoon and Graaf was calling us.

'What, again?' Emmerich groaned. 'What for? So we can freeze to death?'

'Hurry up,' I told him.

'You're kidding,' Emmerich replied. 'Why should I hurry just so I can freeze while I'm

1

standing to attention?'

We felt the same way as him. The whole company did. Why did Lieutenant Graaf need to muster us outside? Wasn't he afraid of the cold, like we were? We could just as easily have heard what he had to say standing by our camp beds here in the warm. Presumably he didn't think it was formal enough, talking to us inside a gymnasium. He'd had a piece of old iron hung from a telephone pole, and we hated the noise it made when it was rung, that sinister chime, even more than the cold that awaited us outside. We had no choice — we obeyed orders — but all the same, it took courage to go out in weather like that.

We had put on our coats, and wound our scarves several times around our necks, tying them behind. Next came the wool balaclava. Completely covered except for our eyes, we went out into the gymnasium courtyard. Bauer, Emmerich and I were the last ones out there.

We were used to it, we knew what to expect, and yet the cold always came as a shock. It seemed as if it entered through your eyes and spread through your whole body, like icy water pouring through two holes. The others were already there, lined up and shivering. While we found our places among them, they hissed at us that we were arseholes for making the whole company wait like that. We said nothing. We got in line. And, when everyone had stopped shuffling their feet to get warm, Graaf, our lieutenant, told us that there would be more arrivals that day, but late probably, so the work was scheduled for the following day, and that this time our company would be taking care of it. I had the same thought as everyone else: was that all? Couldn't he have told us that inside?

Graaf could not tell how it made us feel to know that there would be more arrivals that day. He couldn't see if we were whispering behind our scarves. All he could see was our eyes. And from that distance, he could not yet guess who would report sick the following day.

He hadn't told us how many were coming. He knew it made a difference to us, that it was important. Because if a lot came, he worried that we'd start reporting sick that night.

He nodded, turned around, and went to the officers' mess.

We could have broken rank now and gone back inside, but we didn't. We stayed where we were. Earlier, we would have given almost anything not to have to go outside, and yet we waited before returning to the warm. Perhaps it was because of the work that awaited us the

3

following day. Or because we were already frozen inside, so a few minutes more made no difference.

Now they were outside anyway, the soldiers in charge of the stove that night took the opportunity to fill their buckets with coal. Bauer and I were looking over at the officers' mess because apparently they had a bathtub. We'd been talking about it when the iron sounded. I told Bauer that, in the old days, I'd saved up to have a bathtub fitted. We often used that phrase. We often said 'in the old days', partly as a joke, but not entirely. Emmerich came towards us. He tried not to show us his distress. He had dark rings around his eyes from sleeping during the day.

We went back inside, and sat on Bauer's bed. We didn't talk about the work that awaited us the next day. But because we didn't talk about it, we felt the pressure of it building inside us.

That evening, we asked to see our base commander. What else could we do? We were able to go over Graaf's head because he'd left to see an acquaintance in town — thankfully, as I doubt he'd have let us do it otherwise. The base commander looked away as he listened to us, his hands fidgeting in his pockets as though he were searching for something. We didn't hold back when we spoke to him. He was a bit older than us. In civilian life, he bought and sold fabric in bulk. It was difficult for us to imagine that, though, because for us he had always been some sort of commander.

We weren't telling him anything he didn't already know. Occasionally he would glance towards the door, or give quick little nods. Not because he was in a rush, but because he understood us. We exaggerated a little bit, of course. Here, if you wanted an inch, you always had to ask for a mile. If the cook were to start being a bit stingy with his portions, for example, we would have to say that we were starving to death, otherwise nothing would ever change.

That evening, what we had to say was more important, and our commander gave those occasional nods to show he understood this. We explained to him that we would rather do the hunting than the shootings. We told him we didn't like the shootings: that doing it made us feel bad at the time and gave us bad dreams at night. When we woke in the morning, we felt down as soon as we started thinking about it, and if it went on like this, soon we wouldn't be able to stand it at all — and if it ended up making us ill, we'd be no use to anybody. We would not have spoken like that, so openly and frankly, to another commander. He was a reservist like we were, and he slept on a camp bed too. But the killings had aged him more than they had us. He'd lost weight and sometimes he looked so distraught that we feared he would fall ill before we did and that another, less understanding commander would be appointed in his place: someone we didn't know, or — worse, perhaps — someone we did know. Because it could easily be Graaf, our lieutenant. *He* didn't sleep on a camp bed. He took good care of himself, but not of us. With him in charge, there would be less coal and more marching. With Graaf, we would be ceaselessly filing in and out of the base. When we thought about this, we could hear the iron echoing from dawn till dusk. It went without saying that we liked our commander, no matter how distraught he was.

As usual, he gave us what we asked for, and we left the next morning — Emmerich, Bauer and myself. We went at dawn, before the first shootings. That meant missing breakfast, but it also meant not having to face Graaf, who would be filled with hatred that we had gone over his head. It was still dark, and everything was frozen. The road was harder than stone. We walked for a long time without stopping — in the cold air, under the frozen sky — but we weren't unhappy, in spite of that.

And it was as though I'd lied to the commander the previous evening, because that night, for once, I didn't dream about our life here. I dreamed that Emmerich, Bauer and I took a tram together. It was a perfectly simple dream, but extraordinary for that very reason. The three of us were sitting, and around us all was peaceful and — in contrast with most dreams — entirely realistic. There was nothing to suggest it was false, that the scene existed only in my mind.

I didn't tell Emmerich and Bauer about my dream. I worried that they would start telling me about theirs. Here, good dream or bad dream, the same rule applied: better to keep it to yourself. In fact, why keep it at all, even for yourself?

We went so far without stopping that we couldn't hear anything — not even the echo of the first shots. As cold as it was, we could bear it for the moment. At one point, we thought we could see the sun, but it turned out to be car headlights.

We did not leave the road. We didn't see the point in doing what we'd been sent out to do just yet. A little earlier, we'd gone through a Polish village, drab as a filthy iron plate. At that time, all was still asleep, though we could hear hens clucking somewhere. A chicken would have done us the world of good, that was for sure, but we didn't want to waste time looking for it.

Finally, we saw the pale sun rise. It gave off a little light, but the sky's colour barely changed. It would be noon before it might begin to warm us. And how much warmth it would provide, it was impossible to say.

We could see the horizon now, and dark shapes outlined against it, but that was all. From afar, we could make out forests and hills. The dawning of the new day was like a portent. It was like leaving a place we hated.

We stopped to smoke. Around us was nothing but vast fields. The wind had made waves in the snow, sculpting long, regular shapes that had long since been frozen by the cold. We looked around, and it was as if we were surrounded by a white sea. It was the same up in the sky, except for the eastern horizon where the mist was tinged by the sun.

In the time it took us to light our cigarettes, our hands began to feel burned by the cold. We put our gloves back on. It was a pain in the neck, smoking with gloves on. The gloves were thick. Of course, that was not something to moan about, most of the time. But when we smoked, we moaned about it.

All we could hear was the faint crackle of our cigarettes, our breathing, and occasionally the sound of one of us sniffing back little ice crystals. Smoking on an empty stomach is less pleasant than smoking on a full stomach, but we enjoyed that particular cigarette, all the same. Because the gymnasium and Graaf and the day that was dawning over there were all behind us. We were in the middle of a frozen sea. Around us, everything was ugly and covered in ice, and we were smoking on an empty stomach, but at least we felt safe.

Suddenly Emmerich said: 'I'm afraid he'll start smoking. And what good would it do if I asked him not to do it? Sure, I could write to him that he mustn't smoke, but I don't think it would make a difference. He'd just shove the letter in his pocket and forget about it.'

Emmerich often talked to us like this. He would be thinking to himself, sometimes for quite a while, and then suddenly he would speak his thoughts out loud. It was up to us to quickly grasp the sense of his words, to clamber aboard the moving train of thought. Sometimes we couldn't do it. But this morning, it was fine. We had understood, even before he'd finished speaking, that he was thinking about his son. The boy was one of Emmerich's constant preoccupations. He was plagued by worries about him. We helped him as much as we could. We listened to him for as long as he needed. If he asked us for our opinions, we gave them. We felt sorry for him too: it was tough to see him torment himself like that.

Bauer replied to Emmerich, about the letter: 'You can't know for sure that he'd just shove it in his pocket.'

'Come off it,' said Emmerich, with a faint smile. 'You know perfectly well he would.'

Bauer said, 'Tell him you're coming home, and that he won't be able to hide the smell if he's been smoking, because you'll arrive without warning.'

Emmerich thought about this, making

small movements with his head. We couldn't tell if he was agreeing or disagreeing. Our cigarettes were nearly finished: to make them last as long as possible, we had to remove a glove. Our fingertips burned, from both heat and cold.

I said to Emmerich: 'Tell him we've been given leave, and that it could happen any day now. Don't go into details — just say you might turn up at any moment, and that if he's been smoking, you'll know it as soon as you open the door.'

'But that won't happen,' Emmerich replied quietly. 'So he'd be waiting for me. That would be pretty sad. Each evening, he'd be disappointed.'

Bauer and I glanced at each other. Then I replied to Emmerich, for both of us: 'You're right. Don't tell him that.'

Emmerich managed a brief smile, and wiped his mouth with his hand. Then he stared at his boots. We helped him as much as we could, you see, but we couldn't think of everything.

When we'd finished smoking and tossed the tiny cigarette butts on the ground, we put our gloves back on and pulled our scarves up to our eyes. That was the beginning of a long silence. We stared down at the frozen road and each of us retreated into his own thoughts. I knew what Emmerich was thinking about. With Bauer, it depended on the day.

My own thoughts didn't stray far. I returned to the memory of the previous night's dream, to my tram. But, already, it seemed far away. That's just how it is with dreams. Within a week, it would have vanished into a black hole, where it would remain forever. If only we could put whatever we wanted into that black hole . . .

My back had gone into spasm in the cold, and now it was painful. We started up again, Emmerich in front. Just before we set off, he had let us know, with a shrug of his shoulders and a kind of sigh through his scarf, that he hadn't finished with his problem. So Bauer and I, walking behind him, continued to try to find ways to help him persuade his son not to smoke. Deep down, though, I thought that if he'd decided to smoke, none of us here would be able to stop him. I didn't say that to Emmerich, of course: it would have been like smashing the butt of my rifle into his back.

Bauer and I did not have children. Everyone in the company had them except for me and Bauer. Emmerich had often told us that it was both a boon and a curse; that, before the war, it had been simply a boon, but that now it was a curse as well. We half-understood him.

'Tell him it will bring you bad luck if he does it,' Bauer suddenly shouted.

Emmerich and I jumped. Even through the scarf, the sound was like a rifle shot or the cry of a wild animal.

Our work here had changed Bauer's voice. It exploded without warning. And it had nothing to do with the meaning of his words. He would sometimes start yelling even if what he had to say was perfectly ordinary. Emmerich and I no longer complained about this, not to Bauer and not even to each other. But it still made us jump whenever it happened.

Turning towards us and trembling, Emmerich replied to Bauer: 'If he smoked, and something bad happened to me, his life would be ruined.'

'He's right,' I said to Bauer.

Bauer caught up with Emmerich and touched him on the shoulder. In his true voice, low and thoughtful, he said: 'First something bad would have to happen to you. What could happen to you here?'

'Here? Nothing, I guess,' Emmerich replied. 'We're safe for now. But there's a chance we might be sent somewhere else.'

'Sure,' said Bauer, 'but not tomorrow. And why would anything bad happen to you here?'

Emmerich had slowed down so he could walk alongside us, and he said to Bauer: 'Who knows? Listen, say he smokes, and something bad happens to me — just like that, through chance. What would he do then? I don't want his life to be ruined by chance.'

'That's true,' I said to Bauer. 'He's right.'

Bauer mumbled something behind his scarf. Emmerich said, 'I can't threaten him with that. I'd rather he smoked.'

Bauer lifted up his scarf and said, 'Send him your ration.'

He was talking about his ration of cigarettes. I heard Emmerich give a short laugh. It wasn't very cheerful, but it was better than nothing. And once again, we walked in silence, each lost in our own thoughts. But Emmerich's son walked with us now. Bauer and I didn't know what he looked like. Emmerich didn't have photographs with him. We had never dared ask why. There was maybe some superstition behind it.

While we'd been talking, the sun had continued to rise, and the grey light that it cast on us now was probably as bright as it would get all day. Same for the temperature: you could tell it wouldn't rise any further, even around midday. Thankfully there was no wind. When you thought about it, whenever there was no wind, you could consider yourself happy. For now, the only thing was to be careful where we put our feet. The frozen potholes were dangerous.

I watched the road, lowering my eyes to look out for potholes. Chance, bad luck, Emmerich's concern and love for his son

. . . I was thinking of all this at the same time. But if I had lifted my eyes, if I'd looked away from the road, I mean if it had been possible to see so far, I would have seen where chance lies, the precise location of Emmerich's bad luck . . . I would have seen the bridge in Galicia. I would have seen Emmerich leaning against a pillar, eyes wide open in the warm Galician springtime. I would have heard him pant and spit, trying desperately to speak to us, to Bauer and me, both of us kneeling in front of him. But the blood was choking him, and Bauer and I didn't know what to do with all that blood. And we didn't know how to speak to Emmerich. We didn't know how to do anything at all any more, as if the bullet had gone through us too, without making us bleed like Emmerich, but leaving us crippled, kneeling helplessly before him, useless and silent until the end.

We walked, for a long time. I ended up forgetting Emmerich's son. I ended up thinking only about myself, and time passed differently. We went through another village, asleep like the other one except for one lit window and the smell of smoke.

Sometimes I slipped, and bumped into Emmerich and Bauer. Their contact reassured me. Several minutes after having touched an arm or a shoulder, I still remembered it. I even still seemed to feel it physically.

We came upon a frozen pond. It was the reeds that gave it away, because the ice was white, like the fields around it. It was quite big. On one bank, the wind had blown the snow into a high mound, sharp like the crest of a wave. In the middle of the pond, the frozen reeds indicated the direction the wind had been blowing on the day when everything froze. That day, someone had shoved a stick in the pond.

Bauer told us to wait and went out on the pond. He'd taken his rifle off his shoulder and was using it like a walking stick, to keep his balance.

Emmerich and I walked on the spot to keep warm. We watched Bauer move forward carefully on the ice.

I sensed that we were slowly losing the feeling of happiness we'd had earlier at having escaped work. It wasn't the same now. The day had barely begun, but already it stretched out long and difficult before us. By midday, we would be only halfway through it, whereas back with the company, work might be finished by then. But we couldn't go back so soon, all the same. We would have to wait until nightfall. Because otherwise Lieutenant Graaf would say to us: 'That's too easy, you bastards. This is the last time we let you leave.' From his point of view, he would be right. And the guys in the company would also be right, if they insulted us even more than Graaf did.

If we wanted people to accept our returning early, after work was over, we would have to find some and bring them back. But as yet, we hadn't even started looking. We'd hardly even thought about it.

The only consolation I had left was that there was no wind. If it started up before evening, it would blow away all the relief I'd felt at having avoided work.

Bauer had reached the middle of the pond. He took his rifle in both hands and started smashing the butt against the ice. Shards flew. Bauer kept on. He stopped for a moment and told us, 'It's frozen all the way to the bottom.'

'What did you expect?' Emmerich shouted.

Bauer began again. I yelled to him: 'So, give up. What's the point?'

He looked at me. I felt sure he was smiling behind his scarf. He looked happy. He didn't care what we said. He kept hitting the ice, sending shards flying again. It made a snapping noise. Even from here, you could tell it was frozen all the way to the bottom. There was no need for further verification, if that was why he kept hitting the ice. Nevertheless, he continued. And he put his back into it.

Just as I was about to tell him that he would break his rifle if he didn't stop, Emmerich spoke to me quietly about his son, as if he hadn't wanted Bauer to hear. 'Bad things can happen to us anytime. And then his life would be ruined.'

'That's true,' I murmured. 'You're right. We'll find another solution.'

'Yeah,' said Emmerich, relieved. 'I'd prefer that.'

'We'll find something in the end.'

'I worry I won't manage it on my own.'

'The three of us will give it some thought.'

Emmerich looked at the sky. Not for long.

Just long enough, it seemed, to acknowledge that there were three of us. Perhaps that was Emmerich's consolation, at this particular moment. The helping hand we would give him. Mine was that there was no wind. As for Bauer, perhaps his was to stand in the middle of the pond and examine the thickness of the ice, for reasons that only he knew.

I called him. Then I did it again, louder. It was time we were going. Because, even walking on the spot, Emmerich and I were having trouble staying warm. He came back, walking between the frozen reeds. He took care not to break a single one. He seemed happy about that too. Bauer was more than forty years old, yet he still wanted to make his way between reeds, and doing so made him smile behind his scarf.

He leaped onto the path, and suddenly, out of nowhere, I regretted not having stopped at the lit window earlier to ask for warm milk.

We went on, and soon afterwards I asked why we hadn't thought to demand warm milk in the Polish village. Neither Bauer nor Emmerich could think of an answer. A strange silence followed, and in that silence I saw that they were dreaming about warm milk now, just like I was. They walked with that dream, and it weighed them down. I could almost hear Bauer talking to himself, even though Emmerich was walking between us. As for Emmerich, he tripped and had to hold on to my arm. Their warm milk dreams made mine less painful.

We came to a crossroads and wondered if it wasn't time to consult the map. But it was inside Emmerich's coat, and opening his coat would be like taking an ice bath. In the end, we settled on a path that went south, joking that it would be less cold down there. A pale sun hung in the sky, as distant and useless, it seemed to us, as a coin trapped under thick ice.

Solitary trees stood in the fields. Haystacks too, round and covered with snow, under the aluminium sky. We'd found some of them inside the haystacks during the spring. Not us in particular — Emmerich, Bauer and me — but we knew that some had been found. But there was no point digging in the snow today, in order to search for them. Who would hide in a haystack on a day as cold as this? And the cold had not begun yesterday.

Suddenly Bauer said, 'What if we don't find any?'

'What if we don't?' Emmerich asked.

Bauer imitated the gait of an old man, struggling even more than we were on the road, and said, 'How far do we go before heading back? How long will we stay out here?'

'Let's wait until dark, at least,' Emmerich replied. 'So it looks like we tried.'

'But if the wind gets up,' I added, 'we should go back before dark. Never mind what the others think.'

Bauer sighed that Graaf would kill us if we did that. Half-resigned, half-cheerfully, I said: 'Not as fast as the wind would.'

It was long past daybreak. Finally, we decided to do what our commander had let us leave in order to do. Out of gratitude, more than anything. We felt indebted to him for having allowed us to escape the shootings. So it was time to pay back for what he'd given us. But deep down, we didn't believe it would happen. We didn't expect to find any. Only the gratitude we felt to our commander drove us on to try.

Graaf didn't understand this kind of thing. He didn't know that we could have been better soldiers. He thought that by ringing the iron, he could make us work the way he wanted. But the truth was that, at the slightest opportunity, we did things wrongly, and we were always seeking to get out of the work. When he looked at us, he did not see: 'Give us a little and we'll give you back a lot.' It was no more difficult than that. But, as he saw nothing, Graaf gave nothing — apart from blows on the iron for no real reason at all.

We needed to head towards the woods, towards the forest. In winter, that was the only place they had a chance of surviving, and we of finding them. There was no point searching the Poles' houses any more. The few they'd been hiding had already been caught.

We needed to leave the road now, follow tractor paths and search the forest. There would be no risk of falling in frozen potholes there, but we would certainly sink deeper in the snow. What we gained in stability we would lose in tiredness.

So we took smaller paths. When they led us through woods, we looked between the trees. We searched the air for smoke. Sometimes we went to take a closer look at tracks or something that had caught our eyes between the trees, then afterwards we retraced our steps. The crust of snow gave way beneath our feet, and occasionally we tripped. It's difficult to walk in snow.

We came to a hill, and from there we saw some very clear, deep tracks. They might have been from last night, or the night before, or the night before that. It was impossible to guess how old they were. But in the end, that didn't matter anyway because they went on too far for us to follow. They descended towards a vast plain, utterly white and bare all the way to the horizon. We tried to follow those tracks with our eyes for a while, and then we forgot about them.

But we stayed on the hill. It was time for a smoke. We removed our gloves, and the race against the cold began again. But I had the impression it wasn't as harsh as before. I said to Emmerich and Bauer that it was maybe a bit less cold, that it felt two or three degrees warmer. Bauer lifted his nose and nodded tentatively to acknowledge that this might be true.

We put our gloves back on and we smoked. I didn't dare look at Emmerich. We had not got any further with his problem. I looked at Bauer. Buried in snow up to his knees, he was sitting on the snow crust, which held under his weight, and turned away from the plain. He looked like he was sitting on a chair whose legs had disappeared in the earth. Emmerich seemed less worried than he had earlier. He'd taken off his helmet. His wool balaclava was so tight that it made his face look gaunt. He seemed older. But I would probably have looked older to him too, if I'd taken off my helmet.

Bauer said, 'Apart from getting frostbite, what could happen to us here?'

He was referring to Emmerich's son, of course, and the conversation we'd had before. It seemed a strange idea to bring that back up, even if he was trying to help. I examined

Emmerich's face to see if Bauer's words had sunk him back into his worries, then I signalled to Bauer that there was no point talking about this again. He nodded to show he'd understood, and began looking around. Then, talking about all the wild animal tracks that ran over each other in the snow, he said: 'There must be a lot going on here at night.'

In a peaceful voice, smiling, Emmerich murmured, 'For me too, there's a lot going on at night.'

'You run in the snow at night?' Bauer asked him.

'A little bit, yeah,' said Emmerich.

Bauer turned and pointed out the human tracks that crossed the plain all the way to the horizon, and asked: 'So it was you who did that?'

'Maybe so,' Emmerich replied, smiling again.

Then he nodded to himself. The balaclava really did make his face look strange. But when he smiled, he didn't look so old any more.

As Emmerich had brought the subject up, I lost my head for a second, forgetting that dreams are better kept to yourself, and I said, 'I was on a tram last night.'

Emmerich and Bauer studied me, their expressions asking me silently what on earth I was talking about. 'You two as well,' I replied. 'All three of us were there.'

Bauer shook his head. 'I don't remember that.'

Emmerich looked up at the sky and said, 'If only that were possible, taking a tram at night. We could go and eat somewhere, then come back to sleep in the gymnasium.'

Sitting on his snow chair, Bauer asked, 'Why come back to the gymnasium?'

Emmerich and I agreed with him.

Then we talked about it some more.

I had been right: the cold was less severe than before. To finish our cigarettes, we took off a glove each, and it was less painful than it had been by the frozen pond.

Now Emmerich looked like he was thinking about my tram. I didn't know where it was taking him. He stared at me while he took a drag on his cigarette, which was now so small that I had the feeling he would end up swallowing it.

I inhaled everything I could from mine, too, and gave Emmerich a look that meant I was lending him my tram so he could go and eat somewhere. He didn't understand, of course. It's not easy to give someone a nonexistent tram.

And again, in that moment, if I'd lifted my eyes to the horizon — I mean, again, if it had been possible to see as far as that warm Galician spring — I would have seen Emmerich looking even older than he did now with his balaclava, leaning against the pillar of the bridge. And everything Bauer and I had managed to do, it was almost nothing. The only courage we'd shown was in not turning our eyes away while he panted and spat. But we were so upset, we did not have the courage to touch him or talk to him. And as soon as we stood up, Bauer and I, the mild spring rain began to fall, and we heard it, that rain, on the deck of the bridge. And the two grey curtains it made on either side of us closed us in with Emmerich, with his now dead body and his haggard face, and I knew that we should say a prayer or something. But Bauer looked at me and I looked at Bauer because we no longer dared look at Emmerich and all the blood he'd lost. And for a long time afterwards, to ease my mind, I told myself that the spring rain falling above and beside us, making such a din, had spoken for us. Because, that day in Galicia, someone should have spoken.

We came down from the hill where we had smoked. Bauer whined like a dog that he should never have sat down in the snow, that he felt cold all over now. Emmerich told him to stop, though he said it lightly, not really meaning it. Bauer yelled at us that he'd decided to whine until dark. We found another road and stayed on it for a while. It was a relief not to sink into snow at every step. On the whole, we preferred the frozen potholes, even if they were dangerous.

But eventually we had to go back to the tractor paths that wound their way through snowy woodland.

Just before midday, we stopped to get our breath back and rest our limbs. Bauer looked at the sky and thought he could tell that the weather was going to change, that it would be even colder tomorrow. But I didn't believe him.

I was beginning to feel hungry, but I didn't dare bring the subject up yet. None of us had dared mention it since we left this morning. My stomach ached. Sometimes, when I turned my head too quickly, I felt dizzy. It must have been the same for Emmerich and Bauer.

There was a wood, about two hundred yards away, on the other side of the field, white with frost and really quite beautiful. Emmerich looked at it for a while, and even though we saw no smoke rising and though the snow between here and there was smooth and unmarked, something about it seemed to attract him. Then suddenly he went into the field and began walking across it without saying a word to us.

'Off for a piss?' Bauer joked.

Emmerich paid him no heed. He kept walking away from us. Sometimes the snow held his weight, sometimes it yielded and Emmerich sank up to his knees in it.

'What's got into him?' Bauer asked. 'Where's he going?'

We watched him and waited. We thought he was going to come back. We waited a long time. Two hundred yards is a long way in the snow. Emmerich was struggling to move forward. But he was moving forward — he was moving away from us — and from where we stood, it looked as if he was leaving us. When he had almost reached the edge of the woods, we grudgingly followed his tracks. Bauer moaned out loud, and I moaned in my head. Even where the snow had not yet yielded, it did so under Bauer's weight, and he was walking in front of me. So we crossed the whole field up to our knees in snow. We entered the wood, where we walked another dozen yards before finding Emmerich.

He was crouched in front of the entrance to a hole. He had one hand on a chimney which was barely raised above the ground. It was made from real flue bricks. The snow had melted around it, revealing a circle of dead leaves, pine needles and old, faded scraps of paper.

Bauer and I were so surprised that we needed a moment to ourselves. We contemplated Emmerich's discovery in silence.

Then, patting the flue brick, Emmerich said, 'Look at that. Pretty clever.'

'Well, not that clever really,' I said, 'seeing as we found it.'

'I'm talking about the idea. That's what is clever.'

'Sure, it's a clever idea. But if it had been me, I'd have dug something further from the field, deeper inside the woods.'

Emmerich nodded his agreement. It was strange, but we were whispering.

'How did you find it?' Bauer asked, looking back at the white, unmarked field, towards the path that we'd taken. 'You couldn't see anything from back there.'

'You could, a little bit. There was less frost

on the trees, because of the rising heat.'

Bauer and I looked up at the trees.

We waited for a long time after that. I looked at the chimney that rose above the ground and the circle of melted snow around it. The silence was so profound, it seemed that if we leaned close enough to the narrow entrance in the earth, we might be able to hear breathing down there.

Finally, we called out. Only once, and not very loud. The holes, we knew, were not deep. There were never any tunnels branching out from the main part. He came out soon afterwards, using his elbows, made slow and clumsy by the layers of clothing he was wearing. The top layer, the one we could see, was a town coat with a lined collar. It was misshapen, as if inflated by all the layers underneath.

He stood up and immediately put his hands in the air. We heard nothing — not a word of protest. As if he'd been expecting it. We didn't see anything in his eyes either — no fear, no despair. We could hardly even hear him breathing through his headscarf. All we could see of his face were his eyes beneath his woolly hat. They were ringed with dirt and fatigue, but not enough to hide his youth. Despite the tiredness they showed, they still shone with life.

In that silence, which was almost the same as the silence before we had called him out, we looked at him and smiled behind our scarves. We had been walking since daybreak without believing this would happen, and now Emmerich's sharp eyes had brought him to us. I looked once again at the entrance to the hole, and wondered what had led him to hide here, so close to the edge of the woods, rather than deeper inside them. And I would never know the answer, because I couldn't see how to ask him that question through gestures, nor how he could reply to me.

I signalled for him to lower his hands. Pointing at the entrance to the hole, and using his hands, Bauer asked him if there were any others down there. He shook his head to say no, and we believed him. We did not doubt his word at all.

The sound of wingbeats made us all look up, even the Jew. Frost fell from the trees while a grey shape flew between the branches and vanished. 'It must have been there all this time,' said Bauer.

'We should get out of here too,' said Emmerich.

Until this point, I had stayed crouching in front of the entrance. Now, I stood up. The cold, which I had forgotten, returned, seeping into my back and my legs. The Jew took a step backwards to let me pass. I was so close to him that I noticed a snowflake embroidered on his hat. I looked away and walked, first in line, towards the forest's edge. I didn't know if Emmerich or Bauer had seen the snowflake. I didn't want them to see it now and to start feeling sorry for me.

It was not to make them feel sorry for me that I had, once and once only, told them about this weakness of mine. It was just to tell them, to lighten, momentarily, the weight and sadness I felt whenever I saw that kind of thing — like an embroidered snowflake — on a piece of clothing.

We went back across the field. Standing on the path, Bauer and I looked over at the forest again. It didn't jump out at you — the difference was subtle — but it was true that there was less frost on the trees above the hole.

While we were doing this, Emmerich retrieved the map from inside his coat. He spread it out on the snow. We tried to see where the sun was in the sky, although at this time of day it didn't really indicate west or east. We could just about make it out behind the clouds. We turned the map around so that the cardinal points were in the right positions and we were facing north.

It was difficult to work out where we were. Bauer looked for the frozen pond on the map. If we found that, he thought, we would be able to orient ourselves. 'No way have they put that on the map,' I said. But he looked for it anyway. By chance, we recognised the crossroads where we'd chosen to go south as a joke. We began to understand where we were, and that, if we continued on this path, we would make a loop. We would reach the crossroads more quickly that way than by returning the way we had come.

Emmerich folded up the map, put it back in his pocket, buttoned up his coat, and off we went.

The Jew walked in front, in the old tracks that had frozen. He had fur mittens, better than our gloves. I estimated the thickness of the fur and imagined how warm they must be inside. Then I realised he had his hands above his head again. I told him he could lower them. He understood that I was talking to him, but not what I was saying. He turned around and opened his eyes wide. Using my hands, I signalled to him that he could lower his, and this time he understood.

We were no longer allowed to kill them where we found them, unless an officer was present to vouch for the fact. These days, we had to bring them back. Because it had happened a few times in our company that certain soldiers had come back claiming to have killed them, but afterwards, under Lieutenant Graaf's questioning, it had emerged that either they had not really found any or, if they did find some, they had lost their nerve and let them escape into the forest. In the same way, that day — Emmerich, Bauer and I — we might, without Emmerich's sharp eyes, have gone back to the company at nightfall and sworn on our lives anything we liked. That we'd shot two of them, for instance. How would they know if we were telling the truth? So that was why our commander had been obliged to tell us that we couldn't do it like that any more, and that we always had to bring them back.

Our reading of the map was correct: the path took us to a road, which was where we made our loop, and where the journey back to the base really began. I knew this was the shortest way back, but it was still a long walk. I could feel the cold in my veins now, and I was hungry . . . oh God, yes, now I really was hungry. We were now paying the price for what we'd done this morning: leaving at daybreak, before the first shootings, in order to avoid being seen by Lieutenant Graaf. It was true he hadn't seen us, but neither had the cook. The kitchen had been unlit, the cook still asleep. And the little food we had on us — the slices of bread — we couldn't eat, because it was frozen. The same went for the Italians' cornmeal: we might as well have eaten sand.

Bauer and Emmerich walked in front of me. The Jew was walking faster than we were. The distance between him and us was lengthening.

I strode quickly to catch up with Emmerich and Bauer, and asked them, 'Who's going to shoot him if he starts running?'

'No one,' Emmerich replied. 'We'll run after him, so we can take him back.'

'No,' I said. 'He'd outrun us. I'm sure of it.'

'Well, we'll cross that bridge when we come to it,' said Emmerich.

I don't know why — perhaps for no reason at all, perhaps because I was hungry and tired, and because those feelings made me insecure — but I didn't just accept this. And my voice, I could hear, was harsh and anxious. 'I want to know now. Who is going to do it?'

So Bauer asked me, also in a harsh voice, 'One more or less, what difference would it make?'

It wouldn't make any difference, and we all knew it. But that was not what I was asking them. So I demanded again, 'Who's going to do it?'

Emmerich said nothing. Bauer glanced at me, and said in a voice that sounded false, 'What difference does that make either? I'll do it.'

And he started yelling at the Jew, who had stopped and was watching us from afar. Bauer indicated the distance between him and us, and then beat at the air with his hand. The Jew waited a bit for us to catch him up and then started walking again. Bauer grumbled something to himself. Suddenly, everything changed and I didn't care who shot him. I no longer had that strange feeling, because I'd passed it on to Bauer. To pacify him, I said, 'Or I could do it. I don't mind. I just wanted us to make a decision, once and for all.'

'I'll do it,' Bauer said through gritted teeth. 'It's all the same to me.'

Things were changing fast. Now I felt bad. Bauer was all sullen and miserable. I tried to make it up to him, but I was clumsy and too late. 'Anyway, I'd be surprised if he got away,' I said.

Bauer shot me a look. I decided to keep my mouth shut now.

The house appeared from behind a row of trees. We didn't need to talk about it. The decision was made by our stomachs and the icy sky. We thought about asking for warm milk, coffee, bread or whatever, about sitting down for an hour in the warm, and chain-smoking cigarettes. But as we got closer, even from a hundred yards away, we knew that we weren't going to be asking for anything.

From the outside, it was a filthy little Polish hovel. If any of us had been here alone, in front of it, we would have been scared. If we'd been alone, we wouldn't have stopped. It would have made us uneasy. The roof, covered in ice and snow, looked as though it was pushing the house into the earth. The black wood shutters were closed. A gutter hung loose. The lime between the stones was crumbling. The door was crooked — it had a hinge missing — and it was locked. It took Emmerich several minutes to smash the lock. He hit it with his rifle butt as hard as he could, and it made a sound like when you hit rotten wood. We would have helped him, but we could see he wanted to do it on his own.

The lock finally broke, and we went in, the Jew first. Some house! It was winter in there too, and totally dark, in spite of the door we'd left open. In fact, we almost felt better outside. Emmerich ran out again, as if fleeing for his life. He began smashing the shutters. We heard his rifle butt banging and banging, and something being torn away, and then the light poured in and chased some of the darkness away. When he came back, panting slightly from the effort, Emmerich said, 'So?'

'It's better,' we said.

But as soon as we shut the door, we lost whatever light we'd gained by smashing the shutters. And, as that was the only window, we weren't going to gain any more. But never mind. There was enough light to see what little there was to see.

There was a small whitewashed storeroom, with one door and no windows. I locked the Jew in there. I realised then that he stank like an animal. We'd only caught one, but he smelled bad enough for ten. When I say I locked him in, it's only a figure of speech, because the door didn't close properly. He sat in the back corner and leaned against the wall. He crossed his arms and stared at the floor.

I took my rifle off my shoulder for the first

time that day and put it next to Emmerich and Bauer's, which were leaning against the wall.

In the end, the room grew lighter all by itself. Our eyes adjusted to the darkness, so that we could see well enough. The ceiling was low. There was a trapdoor up to the next floor, but no ladder. The walls had been whitewashed, as in the storeroom, but here they were filthy, covered in soot and damp stains. The furniture was basic: a large table, a bench, two chairs and an empty shelf. Everything that could be carried had been taken away.

Against one wall, there was a stove, like no stove I had ever seen before: tall and wide, in blue enamel. Bauer lifted up the top, and we looked inside. The firebox was deep, like the belly of a great beast. How many logs could we fit in there? On the front was a large mica window. It was covered in soot, but with flames behind it, there was no doubt it would come to life again.

We had a discussion. How long would it take for it to warm up? Should we smoke before we started making a fire, or should we eat? What order should we do it all in?

We were still frozen, and our bread was too. It would have taken courage and strong teeth to eat bread as hard as that. And then we also had the cornmeal the Italians had given us. There wasn't much left — just a bit at the bottom of the small bag — and it took a long time to cook, but each time it was like a miracle seeing how it swelled up, and feeling how nourishing it was.

So it was clear: everything would be better once it was warmer. Smoking and eating in front of the stove! What could be better? We would smoke while we waited for the bread to thaw and for the cornmeal to cook. But the problem was, if there was any wood left, it was outside under the snow, who knew where. It would be dark before we found any.

Emmerich did not hang around. He grabbed a chair, lifted it above his head, and smashed it in a single blow on the concrete slab. He picked up a piece of wood and started cutting it with his knife. He made shavings, taking care that they remained attached to the piece of wood. It would need shavings in order for the fire to take. So Bauer took out his knife and started cutting another bit of the chair.

I looked everywhere for a saucepan. If I didn't find one, we would at least still have our tin mugs. But for the cornmeal, a saucepan would be much better. While I was looking, I caught a glimpse, through the crack in the door, of the Jew sitting on his heels in the storeroom. His legs were spread and he was looking straight ahead. In his layers of clothing, he looked like a huge round bag. His wool hat had been pulled up, revealing his forehead.

I finally found a saucepan behind the stove. It was dirty and blackened, and it had probably been used to empty the ashes. Whoever had been here had taken everything with them except for this saucepan. What would they have done with it? Looking at it now, I felt sure that it had always been used to empty the firebox. I showed it to Bauer and Emmerich, told them to hurry up, and went out to find some snow.

I walked away from the house. I was looking for good, unmarked snow, where no one had walked for a long time before us.

I could see as much snow in the grey and white sky as here on the ground. It was the cold that kept it from falling. That would have been the best snow to melt — no dirt in the water — but of course there was no way of getting it.

I walked past a fence. It was taller than me. Maybe there was a vegetable garden behind it, or maybe I was treading on one at the moment? The wind had blown the snow against it. There was so much, I could use it to wash the saucepan without even bending down. I looked over at the house while I did it. I was waiting for smoke to rise. I was hoping to see flames in the stove when I got back. I threw out the dirty snow and started again. I kept doing it until what I was throwing out was more or less clean. Once again I looked over at the house. Still nothing was coming out of the chimney. What a lot of kindling they must be making! They wanted to be sure that the fire would take with the first match.

I reached the end of the fence. I wanted to go further to collect snow for making the soup. My glove was wet, from having been rubbed against the saucepan. It would freeze soon, and so would my hand.

I turned the corner of the fence, and that was where I saw him, rifle on his shoulder, coming towards me. The Pole halted, and so did I. I hesitated for a moment, but I wasn't scared. If it came down to it, my uniform was at least equal to his rifle. All I could see of him were his eyes; everything else was covered. Those eyes never left me. His dog had joined him, and now it was bounding towards me. It sank in the snow up to its chest and then, with a single thrust, jumped out again. It was incredible, as though something were pushing it up from below. The Pole whistled and the dog stopped moving. It lifted its face towards me. It looked like a nice dog. I noticed little balls of frozen snow hanging from its neck. They were so round, so perfect, that they looked like sleighbells that had been made to decorate its collar. The man whistled again. The dog jumped up — again, it was incredible — and, when it got back to its master, the Pole turned away and retraced his footsteps.

I waited until they'd gone away, and then I collected snow for the soup. I put it in the saucepan, packed it down tightly, and put more in. Snow is bulky. You need a lot of it to make a little water. Experience had taught us that it takes at least five pans of snow to make one of water.

I did not rush. I wanted to give Emmerich and Bauer time to finish their kindling and put it all in the stove. I was still hoping to see smoke rising from the chimney before I went back in the house. But when I turned around, there was nothing to see. If they were waiting for me before lighting it, I had no idea why. I rushed back to the house, giving a yell so they'd know it was me.

Just as I was arriving, the door opened and Emmerich and Bauer came out, running as if pursued by the devil. In fact, they were being smoked out. The smoke poured through the open door and rose up the wall, thick as a wave.

'It's the snow,' Emmerich said with tears in his eyes. 'It's blocked the chimney.'

He walked backwards until he could see the top of the chimney, then said: 'No, it's not the snow.'

'So what is it?' Bauer asked.

'No idea,' Emmerich replied irritably. 'We'll have to look.'

'Go and look,' said Bauer.

Emmerich spat the smoke he'd swallowed

on the ground and said, 'And then what?'

The idea suddenly came to me that the people who used to live in this house had blocked the chimney when they left. Permanently, I mean, with cement. It wouldn't be the first time. So what choice would that leave us? We could make a hole in the roof, or we could go away. We would go, there was no doubt about it. We didn't have the strength to set about doing anything like that.

'What about the Jew?' I asked. 'What shall we do with him?'

'Let's wait till the smoke's cleared a bit,' Bauer replied.

But there was still plenty coming out. Amazing how much smoke a single chair can make!

'Better not wait too long,' I said. 'It'll get in there.'

'Go and fetch him,' Bauer told me.

Emmerich told me the same thing, with his hand. They reckoned they had already swallowed their share of smoke, and now it was my turn. So I went in, and while I was emptying my saucepan of snow into the stove, I called out to the Jew. But I didn't know if he'd heard me, or what he was doing. I couldn't see the storeroom door through all the smoke. When I went out again, my eyes were watering.

After a while, the snow melting in the stove put out the fire. Now it was steam coming out of the house. I went back in. The storeroom door was closed. The Jew had managed to pull it shut. It took all of my strength to open it again. He was crouched in the back corner. There was some smoke here in the storeroom, but not much. It was bearable. He'd taken off one of his mittens and was breathing through it. He looked up at me. I gestured to him, and he stood up and walked out of the storeroom.

Emmerich and Bauer had just come back in and were standing close to the stove. It was still a bit difficult to breathe, but it was better inside than outside. The enamel of the stove had warmed up from the bit of wood it had burned, and the temperature had risen. Not much — one or two degrees — but it made a difference.

Behind us, the Jew started coughing. He couldn't stop. Bauer took him outside while Emmerich and I got to work on emptying the firebox. We took the bits of chair that were still burning and threw them outside, then we examined inside. We were hoping that the chimney was blocked at the bottom, within reach. But everything seemed fine here. I was able to put my arm through the hole, so the smoke could go through it as well.

We had to look higher up. Emmerich helped me to climb on top of the stove.

'You'd better pray that the blockage is here,' I told him.

He closed his eyes. He looked as though he was really praying. I kicked the base of the pipe with my heel a few times. Years of heat and soot had soldered it to the stove. Or maybe it was here that they'd poured the cement. I kicked harder, and the base began to move. I crouched down, grabbed hold of it, twisted it, and lifted it in a single motion. Then, frightened, I let go of it and took a step back, almost falling off the stove. Emmerich caught me, and we looked at one another. He was like me: glad to have found out what the problem was, but disgusted too, and amazed. Of all the things we might have found, I don't think we would ever have guessed at this. A dead cat, head down: that was what had caused the blockage. For a moment, we were mystified, and then we understood. It must have slid in headfirst from the top of the chimney.

I jumped off the stove, and said to Emmerich: 'Take this and toss it outside.'

He grimaced behind his scarf. We were frozen and we were starving, but we were scared of a cat that had been dead for ages.

'Oh, Emmerich!' I said, as if to myself.

He looked at me, but said nothing. Then suddenly he smiled behind his scarf and said, 'You go. I said the prayer.'

His eyes smiled too. The rings beneath them looked smaller and less grey. That was what we'd been missing — a few jokes. Out of gratitude, I picked up the cat in one hand. It was hard and dry as wood, although its fur was still silky. It was a strange, unpleasant feeling, even through the glove. I went outside and threw it a long way to the side of the house, without waiting to show it to Bauer.

The Jew was sitting in the snow just then, wiping his eyes. His mittens were placed on his legs. Next to him, turned away, Bauer was looking at the sky.

'We found it, Bauer,' I said.

'What was it?'

'A cat.'

'A cat!'

'Yeah. We'll have a warm meal tonight, just you wait and see.'

Now Bauer nodded towards the sky. The Jew kept wiping his eyes. I squatted down and picked up the bits of half-burnt chair that we'd thrown out.

Bauer was sitting on the bench, the Jew had returned to the storeroom, and Emmerich and I were taking care of the fire. But the wood from the chair had hardened when it burned, and now it was impossible to cut shavings from it. I went outside and brought back the shutter that Emmerich had broken off in order to let some light into the house. I broke the shutter into smaller bits. It was easier to cut shavings from that wood.

As soon as the wood had begun to take, and the flames were dancing behind the mica window, I went back outside with the saucepan, to the same place I'd been before. I packed the snow tightly into it, then added more and packed that down too. I noticed the tracks made by the Pole and his dog. They went off a long way — who knew where? I kept staring off into the distance. The earth was white. Not long ago, it had been yellow. It had been covered in sunflowers.

When I turned around, there was smoke floating from the chimney. The sight lifted my heart. Added to the fact that we had avoided the shootings and that there had been no wind since the morning, it was no exaggeration to say that this had been a good day.

And of course Emmerich's sharp eyes had made it an even better day, for tomorrow we would undoubtedly avoid the shootings again, if there were any. Bringing one back meant we would have the right to go out searching again. Nobody would be giving us evil looks. Even Graaf would not be able to find anything to reproach. Tomorrow morning, we would be able to walk past him without lowering our gaze. Unlike today, we would even be able to wait for the kitchen to open so we could get our rations. We would be entitled to all of that tomorrow.

The hunger made me dizzy, and the cold hurt my bones, but I was now thinking that today would end up being even better than my tram dream. I went back to the house with my spirits raised by these thoughts, and when I entered they rose even higher, because the temperature was now above zero. It was already quite warm. Emmerich and Bauer had put their helmets on the table. They un-wound their scarves and removed their balaclavas. I placed the saucepan on the stove and did the same. Finally, my face could breathe. I rubbed my cheeks and ears and the back of my neck. Blood flowed back into the veins. We hung our scarves and balaclavas on the metal bar that ran around the stove.

Then we put the frozen slices of bread on the edge, so that they would thaw without burning, and we moved the bench in front of the stove. Emmerich and I sat down. Bauer remained standing, and watched us. He looked as if he was guarding us. 'What's up, Bauer?' I asked.

He smiled thinly. His balaclava had left blue lines on his cheeks. He pretended to look away. I decided to let it drop. If there was something on his mind, we would find out soon enough.

In accordance with the plan for the day we'd worked out earlier, it was now time to smoke. We had been right to wait. It was the best cigarette of the day. We weren't wearing gloves any more and we didn't need to rush. The cold was outside. And because of the smell of the burning wood, it tasted good, despite our empty stomachs.

I got up to see what was happening with the snow in the saucepan. It was beginning to shrink and turn clear. I was worried, though: the shutter was burning quickly.

How cheerful the flames looked behind the mica window! There would be enough wood to thaw the bread, but not to cook the cornmeal soup. No doubt the bench where Emmerich and I were sitting would end up being burned too, but I decided to wait, and not to mention it yet. I wanted to finish my cigarette in peace, down to the very end.

Bauer kept watching us, smoking with a strange expression on his face. Without looking at him, I said, 'What do you want, Bauer?'

Suddenly, his voice mysterious, he whispered, 'Who's the best of us three?'

To begin with, we waited and said nothing. Then Emmerich asked: 'In what sense, and why?'

'Yeah,' I added. 'In what sense, Bauer?'

Bauer did not reply.

'If you're talking about the best character,' I said, 'then you've lost.'

Bauer remained impassive, letting his mysterious question hang in the air. He was pretending to wait for an answer that was impossible to give. But Emmerich and I were waiting too. It would come, we knew. During this moment of silence, the Jew coughed in the storeroom. He had been coughing before, but now, strangely, in the warmth of the house, it felt as if we were hearing him for the first time.

Our cigarettes were burning down to the end. One or two more drags. We would remember this smoke.

'Bauer, if you want to know who's the

best,' Emmerich said suddenly, 'it's because you think it's you.'

'Maybe,' said Bauer.

He clicked his tongue. We looked up at him. And then, from one of his coat pockets, he produced an onion, and from the other a lump of lard. Now we were watching him wide-eyed. The show was not over. From the inside pocket of his coat, he took out half a salami, and moving in slow motion, he placed it on the table, between Emmerich and me. It wasn't some soft, disgusting liver sausage either, but real salami.

'Keep going,' I said.

'That's your lot,' Bauer replied.

'And the potatoes?' I joked.

In the same spirit, Bauer replied, 'Didn't find any.' But then, more seriously, he added: 'This will be some soup, though. You'll see.'

We had no trouble believing him. Already, we could smell the salami, tickling us between the tops of our jaws and our ears, making us drool.

But as happy and drooling as we were, Emmerich and I, we were not entirely surprised. The salami was not exactly an unexpected gift that had fallen from the sky.

Because Bauer, despite being over forty years old, often stole things. He was prone to strange compulsions, and did strange things.

He still had certain characteristics that Emmerich and I had lost, probably because Emmerich was a father, and as for me . . . well, that's life. Emmerich and I would never have tried to see if the pond was frozen all the way to the bottom by smashing at it with a rifle butt. Sometimes we were bothered by what went through Bauer's head. Sometimes it frightened us. We feared he would get us into trouble.

And because we feared it, it came to pass.

One day, when Kropp the cook was bawling him out for stealing, he yelled back, 'Go fuck yourself — you're the thief!' and Emmerich and I got in as much trouble as Bauer did, as if we were his accomplices. And Bauer knew you had to be careful with Kropp.

Kropp was touchy. Not a bad guy, but a bit of a loner and very sensitive. After the first killings, he had said, 'I'm not doing that.' He'd left the clearing where it was taking place, he'd gone back towards the trucks, and he'd said, 'Give me something else to do. I'll bring food, I'll bring drink, I'll clean the trucks, whatever you want. I don't care. But I'm not doing that.'

Everyone got their hands dirty that day. Nearly all of us suffered. But not him. So everyone cursed him. He took the brunt of the company's hatred and contempt. Some wanted to beat the shit out of him. It nearly happened. Graaf wanted to kill him. And he would have done. But the commander intervened. 'Who will pay for this?' Kropp asked him. The commander didn't answer, but he was an understanding, accommodating man, and he arranged for Kropp to be sent to the kitchen to replace the real cook, who had jaundice. That saved Kropp's bacon, and he remained the cook. And after that, people had to stop cursing him, of course, because he was the one filling our mugs and our plates. Because it was up to him how much broth and salami and bread we got.

So that's why, sometimes, we weren't too mad about Bauer's ideas. But today, with the salami . . . well, we weren't about to spit on that.

The only problem was that, with all of the food we had now — the onions, the lard, the salami, and the cornflour that takes so long to cook — I was getting even more worried about the wood.

I got up and glanced at the snow in the saucepan. It had almost melted. Soon it would be water, though barely even luke-warm. I shoved what remained of the shutter into the firebox and told the others: 'There won't be enough wood.'

59

'We need coal. They wouldn't have been able to take that with them.'

If there were any, it would be in the storeroom. Was it possible I hadn't seen it? I didn't think so, but I went back anyway. I pulled the door open and was instantly hit by the icy air and the stink. The Jew, sitting on his heels, lifted his head and looked at me. His wool hat had been pushed further back, uncovering his ears. I felt hatred rising up in me for the snowflake embroidered on it. All the more so as I'd forgotten about it until then. I turned away from it and examined every inch of the storeroom, lifting up bags and old newspapers with my foot. Beneath lay frozen earth, and not a single piece of coal. Not even the hint of one. 'There's nothing in here,' I shouted.

'What about outside, behind the house?' Emmerich asked.

'No, that's impossible,' I replied.

I came back out, and while I was pushing the door shut so I wouldn't have to see the wool hat any more, Emmerich said, 'Leave it a bit open.'

'What for?' I asked, although I knew.

'He'll freeze,' said Emmerich. 'What good would that do us?'

'He won't freeze any more in there than he would in his hole.'

'Leave it a bit open anyway.'

The Jew watched me. He knew we were talking about him. I went out of the storeroom, leaving the door half-open.

Next, we worked out how much wood was left. There was one chair, the bench, the shelf and the table. We felt remorseful at the thought that it would all have to be burned, though. Bauer pointed to the trapdoor that led to the attic. 'Why don't we look up there?'

We pushed the table underneath it and put the chair on top. But who would climb up? It wasn't very high, but you had to hoist your entire body weight up on your elbows. Thankfully, Emmerich had already taken off his coat. He climbed onto the table, then onto the chair, and he lifted up the trapdoor as he was standing up. It was heavy. It made a very loud noise as it fell onto the attic floor. Everything shook, and black dust fell down on us. Emmerich leaned on his elbows and, using all his strength, grunting and moaning, lifted himself up. To help him, Bauer and I seized one leg each and pushed him towards the ceiling. Finally, he managed to get one knee inside, and then the other. He moaned again, and then he was in the attic. Crouching down, he got his breath back and looked down at us. His whole body shivered. 'It's still freezing up here.'

'So hurry up!' Bauer told him.

Emmerich turned his head. 'It's completely dark.'

'You want your rifle?' Bauer asked.

Emmerich half-smiled, half-grimaced, then stood up and disappeared into the darkness.

While we waited, we sat with our backs to the stove, Bauer on the table and me on the bench. We could hear Emmerich walking around the attic. We tried to guess where he was. Bauer shouted up at him: 'Go on! Keep at it!'

Emmerich made some vague reply, and Bauer yelled: 'Think about the salami!'

'I'm not thinking about anything. I can't see anything either.'

'Use your lighter!'

'You think I haven't?'

'If he doesn't find any,' I said to Bauer, 'we can burn the trapdoor.'

Bauer, instantly struck by this idea, clapped his hands and shouted: 'Come back down! We've found something!'

Emmerich reappeared above the hole. He crouched down at the edge. 'A mattress, some rotten apples . . . I walked in them,' he said. 'But no wood. So what did you find?'

'The trapdoor,' Bauer told him.

'Of course!' Emmerich nodded. 'Why did I bother looking inside?'

'Go on, try it. Pull on it.'

Emmerich grabbed hold of it, lifted it up and tried to twist the hinges. But they held.

'Come and help me! I can't do this on my own.'

Bauer climbed up on the table, then on the chair, and the two of them pulled hard at the trapdoor, swearing and grunting like animals. I went up there to help them, but just as I did, the trapdoor gave. Bauer sent it hurtling to the ground, and it only just missed me. It cracked on the concrete floor, and a split appeared in the wood. So while Bauer helped Emmerich to come back down, I went to work on the trapdoor. But it was heavy and thick and still very solid. It was difficult to chop it into bits. But never mind, I thought — it would take longer to burn like this. I kept smashing away, though, and eventually managed it, making a reassuring woodpile next to the stove.

The snow had melted in the saucepan by now. The water was beginning to steam. We needed more snow. I asked Bauer and Emmerich for their tin mugs, tied my now-warm scarf around my neck, and went back outside. The cold fell on me like a sledgehammer. The sky too, or so it seemed, as if it were now lower than before, all grey and white. Sky and earth had blurred into one, and there was no comfort to be found in either. While I packed the snow into our mugs, I wondered again how it was possible that we had once seen so many sunflowers here, and not so long ago either. The landscape had been so full of them, so completely covered, that it seemed their oil must have been flowing like a river somewhere. We could have done with some for our soup. Instead of oil, we had lard, which was poor stuff in comparison. Today, though, it seemed like gold. Today, what we missed was not the oil from the sunflowers but their bright yellow light.

I had not put my gloves back on. I packed the snow in the mugs and my fingers hurt so much that for the last mug — mine — I just shoved the snow in with a single movement, not even bothering to pack it down. Then I ran back to the house. Without the balaclava and the helmet, the silence was like a sharp stone.

The snow I'd brought back in the mugs had melted, and the saucepan was just over half-filled. The water was steaming again. We were getting there now. Emmerich and I were on the bench, Bauer standing in front of the stove. He cut the onion in four and threw it in the saucepan. The lard, he dropped in whole. Next, he added the cornmeal. All we had to do now was wait. I looked at the salami, which was still sitting on the bench between Emmerich and me. Bauer had not forgotten it — he was thinking about it too — but he was taking his time to reach a conclusion.

Finally, I asked: 'What about the salami?'

Bauer hesitated. 'What shall we do?' he asked dreamily. 'Shall we eat it or shall we wait?'

Emmerich and I became dreamy too. After a while, I said, 'Is it frozen?'

'No,' Bauer replied. 'It was pressed against me.'

But, just to check, he picked it up from the bench. He squeezed it and sniffed it.

'It's fine,' he said. 'What shall we do?'

'Why don't we put it in the soup as well?' Emmerich said.

'All of it?' Bauer asked.

'Why not?' said Emmerich.

But I was sick of waiting. I needed to eat something now. So I said, 'Or we could cut it. Eat a bit now, and put the rest in the soup.'

It was Bauer's decision. He had brought the salami. We would all eat an equal share, that was certain, but it was up to him to decide the way in which we ate it.

'All right,' he shouted suddenly.

We jumped. But we didn't know what he was agreeing with. He took his knife out and, on the bench, cut the salami into twelve thin slices, so perfectly equal that we could have chosen one with our eyes closed. He dropped six slices into the soup and we helped ourselves to the others.

There was nothing left to discuss now. Each of us had two slices, and we could do what we liked with them. Would we eat them straight away? Would we keep them to eat with our bread when it was warm enough? Or did we have enough will power to wait for the soup to cook, so we could eat it all at the same time?

I didn't even have time to think about it. One of the slices was already in my mouth, and the second followed it soon afterwards.

Emmerich and Bauer had scoffed theirs too. And if we'd followed our instincts, we'd have fished the other slices out of the saucepan and eaten those too. The taste of it that remained in our mouths felt so good, yet at the same time it was torture. We couldn't stop drooling, and wanting more.

Before he sat down with us on the bench, Bauer dipped a finger in the soup and said, 'Lukewarm.'

I couldn't believe it. 'Only lukewarm?'

'Yeah.'

I glanced at what remained of the trapdoor: barely half of it.

'If it's only lukewarm now, we're going to have to burn everything, including this,' I said, tapping the bench.

'Never mind,' said Bauer. 'We'll burn everything, then. I'm hungry. The table, too. Who cares?'

He sat down between us. That is the difference between wood and coal. Wood burns fast.

We smoked another cigarette because there was nothing else to do, apart from watching the fire in the stove. The window had quickly frosted over and no longer let much light through. The flames behind the mica window lit us up like an electric bulb.

And, because there was nothing to do now

but wait for the soup, I sensed that Emmerich was quietly withdrawing into himself, and I knew what he was thinking about, which problem he was once again struggling with in his mind. Bauer knew too, and he nodded to me discreetly, just between the two of us. I replied in the same way. We were sorry for Emmerich, but what could we do?

The three of us were silent. We smoked without speaking. But Emmerich's silence was different to ours, and Bauer and I could feel it. His silence grew ever thicker. But only from the outside, because inside his head, his son was making so much noise — knocking hard on the door of his conscience — that Bauer and I could hear him. So how loud the din must have been inside Emmerich's head. I remembered that the three of us were supposed to think about his problem together. I'd promised him that as we stood by the frozen pond. He probably didn't dare remind me of this. He was probably waiting for me to say something. But I wanted to smoke first.

The Jew started coughing again. I turned round to look. He was sitting with his legs folded under him. The temperature had risen inside the storeroom too: he had opened his coat. Underneath he was wearing a thick quilted jacket. And even though, from here, I could not see the snowflake embroidered on his hat, I thought about it anyway, though distantly and not for long.

Yes, I felt like finishing my cigarette before helping Emmerich. It was peaceful, smoking in front of the stove. I wanted to savour that moment until it was over. That was why I waited. But I knew there was also a bit of spite in it. Because there had been times when I'd needed help too.

You could smell the rotten apples. They'd stuck to Emmerich's boots when he came down from the attic. They smelled almost like jam. Oh, if only we'd had some jam to eat after the soup! Emmerich got up and turned the bread over on the edge of the stove, then sat back down. And, once again, I heard his son knocking.

It was not the first evening, nor the second, but the third evening after the first shootings that Emmerich started fearing for him. And since then, the fear had never left him. It was probably his son that Emmerich saw when he stared at Bauer and me, later, in the spring, while he was dying under the bridge in Galicia. No, in truth I don't know if it was him that Emmerich saw when he looked through us. But I hoped it was him, so that he could have seen him one last time while he died, to help him. And, through hoping, I ended up believing it.

But on that evening — the third after the first shootings — we came back from outside, where Graaf had called us, the whole company, for no good reason: to tell us about some coal that had been stolen and sold to a Pole. Emmerich had sat on his bed, face pale, and sighed pitifully, then told us — Bauer and me — about his son, with such intensity in his voice that we didn't dare take off our coats, as if by doing so we would have deprived him of something.

We listened to him. He had a lot to say.

Emmerich had been holding this in for three days. We understood that the distance between his home and our base here in Poland had grown longer, stretched out. It was almost as if a wall had risen up between them.

Like everyone else, Bauer and I were still living through the shootings, the killings; they flashed endlessly before our eyes and reverberated in our ears. So much so that listening to Emmerich talking so helplessly seemed strange to us. Could we tell him that? But thankfully, he was not asking us for advice, at least not yet. We listened to him. We understood him and we did not understand him and we were too hot in our coats, and after three days the killings were still filling up our minds, boiling away inside them, and spilling over. And on top of this, all Emmerich's fears for his son, instead of making us forget our own worries, just made them worse.

We had never thought about his kid before then. We knew he existed, and that was all. He'd talked about him, of course, the way friends always talk to each other about their wives if they're married or their children if they have any. But from that evening on, Emmerich's son became part of our lives. He was, so to speak, sitting on Emmerich's bed.

He slept with us that night, and every night after, and he was there with us every morning too, at breakfast. It was as if Emmerich had caught a disease.

After that evening, Emmerich managed to use each event here to talk to us about his son. Not only about his fears, thankfully, but also memories, details. And that was fine. But it was a real disease, all the same. Sometimes Bauer and I couldn't stand it any more. And we told him so.

The fire soon died down. I got up and filled the firebox with the wood from the trapdoor. There was enough left to fill it again, but only one more time. So Emmerich got up too, picked up the second chair and smashed it on the concrete slab, so hard that bits of wood flew everywhere. We could see that what he was trying to smash was his problem as much as the chair. He collected the bits and, before sitting down, dipped his finger in the soup.

'It's slightly warm,' he said.

'At this rate, what we eat will be hot but not cooked,' said Bauer in a resigned voice.

'There's a fence outside,' I said. 'But it's covered in snow. We'd never get to it.'

'If only there were coal,' Bauer said, 'that would be perfect. We could sleep, and when we woke up it would be cooked.'

I looked around me. There was still the shelf. After that, we'd have to burn the bench, and after the bench, the table. But then where would we eat? The concrete slab was still frozen. We'd have to eat standing up.

'What we eat will be cooked,' I said, 'but

we'll eat standing up. It's not the end of the world.'

I sniffed at the steam that was rising from the saucepan. The flavour was starting to form. The onion and the salami tickled my palate. The cornmeal was still at the bottom: it had not yet begun to swell. That was what we were waiting for. But maybe the shelf and the bench would be enough, and we would still have the table to eat from. I went back to the bench and sat down. After a while, Bauer's head started to drop and then he sat up straight. He was gradually falling asleep like that. I would have liked to do the same.

Suddenly I thought about our rifles that were leaning against the table behind us. What if the Jew crept out of the storeroom? I turned my head and glanced at him through the opening. He hadn't moved. Bauer began breathing through his nose. He would end up falling fast asleep, even without coal in the stove to reassure him. Emmerich was fiddling with a button on his coat. The waiting and the warmth of the stove were sending each of us into our own little worlds.

That was why I stood up and went outside. I didn't go far. I stayed on the threshold, under the eaves. With the stove radiating heat behind the door, and the saucepan steaming, the house seemed a bit less like a filthy Polish hovel.

A thin shower of snow fell from the roof in front of me, sparkling like silver. It was so light that I couldn't even feel the wind that had lifted it off the roof. There must have been some sunlight, too, to make snowdust sparkle like that, but I couldn't see the sun anywhere in the sky. I waited for another snow shower, without quite knowing why. But it was smoke from our fire that floated past my eyes.

The snowflake on the Jew's hat was now tormenting me. It had followed me outside. It had come with me, in my thoughts. It had been there more or less constantly since the Jew had emerged from his hole, and I no longer had the strength to drive it away. All my strength had been drained by hunger and tiredness. I didn't dare talk about it again to Emmerich or Bauer, I suppose because it was not the kind of torment that had me on my knees. When I looked at it directly, it was bearable. For that reason, I didn't dare ask them for the help I needed.

It had seemed so unlikely that we would find one. But chance, being chance, had brought us one wearing something with the power to cause me pain. I had come outside to forget it a bit, but that hadn't worked. All I had found was the cold silence of winter.

I laughed bitterly to myself at the thought

that perhaps this snowflake was tormenting me for nothing. Perhaps it wasn't his mother who had embroidered it? He might just have bought the hat, with the snowflake embroidered on it in a factory. There might be hundreds of other people who had worn the same one, who were wearing it even now.

Because if you want to know what it is that tormented me, and that torments me to this day, it's seeing that kind of thing on the clothes of the Jews we're going to kill: a piece of embroidery, coloured buttons, a ribbon in the hair. I was always pierced by those thoughtful maternal displays of tenderness. Afterwards I forgot about them, but in that moment they pierced me and I suffered for the mothers who had, once, gone to so much effort. And then, because of this suffering they caused me, I hated them too. And the more I suffered for them, the more I hated them.

And if you want to know more, my hatred knew no bounds when they were not there to hug their darlings tightly to their breasts while I killed them. Once, they had embroidered a snowflake on their hat or tied a ribbon in their hair, but where were they when I was killing them?

Someone called my name. It was Bauer. I went back in, looked inside the saucepan, and sat down again on the bench. The flames were still high behind the mica window.

'It'll end up being cooked,' Bauer told me.

'I think so too.'

Then I said, 'Why did you call me?'

'I don't know!' he yelled in my ear.

I waited, hesitating, still not daring to ask for help. Better to do something else. So I said to Emmerich, about his son: 'Listen, don't make any threats. Tell him kindly what you think. Be honest and tell him what you told us — that it really bothers you to imagine him smoking. Listen, be direct about it. Don't beat around the bush. Tell him you'll be pleased if he doesn't smoke.'

Emmerich leaned over and shot a look at me. His eyes glistened slightly. He was even smiling — not sadly, but sincerely.

'I'd be happy, not just pleased,' he said.

'There you go, even better. Tell him you'll be happy. I swear to you, he won't be able to refuse you that.'

His smile widened. He rubbed one hand over his head, then the other one. After that, he didn't know what to do with his hands, so he stared at them. He looked as though he was going to put them together.

'Do it, Emmerich,' I whispered. 'Don't be afraid to tell him.'

'Yes, yes,' Emmerich replied, lifting his eyes up.

'It's better like that, don't you think?' I asked Bauer. 'Instead of threatening him.'

Bauer moved his head to one side, and then the other.

'This is a good way of doing it,' I insisted. 'In fact, it's the only way, really — to show his trust in him.'

'Yeah, why not?' Bauer said. I could tell he was not entirely convinced, but he said it to please Emmerich.

Thankfully Emmerich didn't notice, and suddenly, quietly, as if to himself, he said, 'It's funny, isn't it, because us three, here, we'd die if we couldn't smoke.'

Put like that, what he said was so strange and true that we felt a bit disoriented, and stayed silent. And while each of us was dealing with that, as best we could, there was a knock at the door.

All three of us jumped, but we didn't even have time to say a word, because the door was pushed open immediately afterwards. It was the Pole, the hunter, who I'd seen earlier, while I was collecting snow. His dog came in with him. The Pole crossed the threshold and shut the door behind him. The dog moved towards us. He still had those little balls of snow hanging on his neck. The Pole took his rifle from his shoulder and leaned it against the door, then moved towards the stove as calmly as if he were in his own home. And for a moment, forgetting he'd knocked, I believed that we really were in his house, sitting in front of his stove.

'What do you want?' Bauer asked him.

The Pole did not reply. Bauer grunted louder: 'What do you want?'

The Pole signalled — as if he were sorry, but not very sorry — that he didn't understand. We believed him. But that didn't alter the fact that he was facing up to us, in spite of his somewhat apologetic demeanour. He was leaning with one hip against the stove, calm and impassive, just as if he were at home.

Sitting on the bench, we looked up at him, and began to smile at the desire he had — we understood this now — to show us he was not afraid of us. Because we didn't care if he was afraid of us or not.

'I know him,' I said. 'I saw him outside.'

'What's his name?' Bauer asked me. And to amuse himself, he asked the Pole, 'Have you come to eat? You'll have to wait a while. It's not cooked yet.'

Then he pretended to make a space for him on the bench, between us.

'Come and sit down while you wait.'

The Pole remained motionless. Only his eyes moved, sparkling shyly like a wild animal's, in reply to Bauer's honeyed tone.

But while this was going on, the flames had begun to die down. I got up and filled the firebox with what was left of the chair. As I did this, I observed the Pole. He didn't look at me, not even sideways. Bauer, who also noticed the way the Pole was ignoring me, as if I worked for him, said to me, 'Do it properly for him.'

And to the Pole, about me, he said: 'Tell me if he doesn't do it right, I'll have a go at him for you.'

The Pole frowned at Bauer, then sniffed behind his scarf.

I went back to sit on the bench. The Pole watched us. From where we sat, his eyes looked like coal. He removed his animal-skin hood, edged with thick fur, then he unwound his scarf, which was long. We saw his face. I was struck by how distinguished he looked. He must have been about forty, like us. Then he opened his mouth, and it would have been easier to count the teeth that remained than those he'd lost. But he wasn't disfigured by his toothlessness. His face kept its seriousness, and that shy, distinguished look that we didn't often see in Poland.

He put his hood in a pocket, and then found a space for his scarf between ours on the metal bar that ran around the stove. He took his time, hanging it carefully, and while he was doing that, we no longer saw the flames, and it was as if we felt less warm.

'You're a Catholic,' Bauer told him, 'so fuck off out of here.'

The Pole understood that. He went back to the side of the stove, and at that moment his dog — I don't know where it had been — came suddenly from behind us, rubbing itself against us, and lay down next to him. He spoke to it without looking at it. The dog put its head on its paws. I pointed the little dangling balls of snow out to Emmerich and Bauer. 'Look at that,' I said.

'I've seen that before,' said Emmerich. 'I don't know how it happens, but I saw it before one day.'

'Where?' Bauer asked.

'Where? At home.'

'Just like that? Exactly the same?'

'Yeah. Why?' Emmerich asked.

Bauer started to laugh.

'Why are you laughing?' Emmerich asked.

Bauer was alluding to Emmerich's testicles. I'd got the joke. Emmerich asked him again why he was laughing. But with the flood of laughter pouring from his mouth now, Bauer couldn't reply. He even had to stand up, because his sides were hurting. Suddenly Emmerich nodded. The penny had dropped.

He smiled from ear to ear.

After a while, Bauer began to calm down, and he wiped the tears from his cheeks. He opened his mouth, but then his body was gripped by little shudders and it looked as if he was about to start up again. If Emmerich had said anything, he would have done. Emmerich knew that, and kept silent. So Bauer finally calmed down completely. He opened his mouth and took a deep breath. And, as he was already standing, he took the opportunity to check on the soup. He unsheathed his knife and stirred it with the blade, eyeing the Pole at the same time.

'So, you other Poles,' he said, 'you're doing all right, are you?'

The Pole said something in reply. He sounded serious, his voice deep and calm. At his feet, the dog raised its head.

'Without a doubt,' Bauer said, never taking his eyes off him.

Then he stuck the knife in the saucepan and, at the first attempt, picked up a slice of salami, which he wafted under his nose and put back in the soup.

'What about the cornmeal?' I asked. 'Is it cooking?'

He put away his knife, took out his spoon, and gave the soup a good stir, watching the cornmeal to see if it rose to the surface or if it

84

was starting to thicken at the bottom. He shook his head and licked the spoon.

'No, not yet,' he said. 'When I stir it, it floats. But it's starting to cook a little bit.'

'Let me see!'

He drew out a spoonful and, being very careful not to lose a drop, moved it towards me. But I didn't inspect the consistency of the cornmeal, I just swallowed the whole spoonful. Bauer was right: it wasn't cooked. But it was hot and it tasted good. Grudgingly, I told him, 'Yeah, I agree. Needs a bit more time.'

I held back from saying that it was cooked enough, that the consistency of the cornmeal didn't matter any more. I was hungry, so terribly hungry. We had eaten yesterday evening, but yesterday seemed as long ago as last month.

'And the bread?' Emmerich asked.

Bauer turned around, stuck his finger in one of the slices, and said, 'The bread's fine.'

'What shall we do?' Emmerich asked.

'Same as for the salami. Everyone can decide for themselves,' Bauer replied.

We waited, looking at one another. If we ate our bread now, the meal wouldn't be as good, it wouldn't be complete. But we were so hungry. What to do? Finally, we decided, without anything being said, that we would eat it all together, the bread and the soup when it was cooked. Bauer sat back down with us. He started examining the Pole.

'Why don't we chuck him out?' he shouted suddenly.

The Pole jumped. He stared hard at Bauer. Then, from a chest pocket, he calmly took out a large green half-litre flask. It was potato alcohol, we knew. Everyone round here had it. It fell like rain from those large flasks. Straight away, we wanted some. He unscrewed the lid and moved towards the soup. He did all of this without taking his eyes off us, and when he tilted his head back slightly and opened his eyes a little wider, we understood what he meant. He wanted to buy a share of our meal by pouring the alcohol into the soup.

Before talking about it, we spent a moment imagining how good it would feel.

'What do you think, Bauer?' I asked. 'It's your soup.'

'Why not?' said Bauer.

He turned towards Emmerich.

'I definitely want some,' Emmerich replied.

'All right. Hang on a minute,' said Bauer.

He looked at the ground, deep in thought. The Pole watched us, patient and impassive. His flask was still suspended over the saucepan.

'We'd have less soup,' said Bauer. 'But I do want some of that.'

'Go for it,' I told him.

'It doesn't matter about there being less soup?'

Emmerich and I shook our heads: it didn't matter. Bauer asked, 'What flavour will it have?'

We told him it would be better. But he still seemed unsure. I didn't know why. I was wishing we hadn't told him it was his soup, even if it was true.

'The bread,' he said. 'Are we letting him have some bread too?'

'No,' I replied. 'Only the soup. We keep the bread for ourselves.'

Bauer bent over and lifted his head.

'All right, go ahead then, my good fellow,' he said to the Pole, gesturing with his hand. 'And put lots in.'

We'd known it was going to happen. From the moment the Pole took the flask from his pocket, it had been almost certain that we would have some. But still, it was a huge relief, watching him pour it in. He poured in a lot. We heard the alcohol boil, we saw it evaporate, and — almost instantly — we caught its smell.

That smell made us smile, but it caused us pain too. If only the smell alone could fill our bellies . . . But you can't eat air. In spite of the pain, though, we were smiling, all except for the Pole. His handsome toothless face watched us with the same serious, impassive expression it had worn since he entered the house.

Bauer nodded to him. 'That's not all. Come over here and look. Our soup is going to be magnificent, but it'll cost you.'

The Pole moved towards him and carelessly handed him the flask, not even looking as he did so. As I already said, this stuff fell like rain in Poland. Bauer drank a mouthful, gasped like a horse, then passed the flask to Emmerich. He gasped like a horse too, and moaned with pain. And while I, in turn, burned my throat, the Jew sniffed and coughed in the storeroom, as if he were the one who'd just drunk the alcohol.

The Pole took a step forward, almost touching us, then looked inside the storeroom, through the half-opened doorway. Because, up to this point, the Jew, though very close, had been invisible to him. The Pole stayed there now, motionless in front of us, staring with his black eyes at the squatting Jew, who stared sadly back. After a moment, the Pole turned his gaze on us, and the distinguished handsomeness of his face vanished. He opened his mouth and bared his gums in a kind of monstrous smile, like a dead fish without teeth.

He looked at the Jew again.

'What's up with you?' Bauer asked. Then, a few seconds later: 'What did you see that made you grin like that?'

The Pole seemed unwilling to stop staring at the Jew, and his peeled-back lips expressed a sort of satisfaction. Bauer demanded, 'What's got into you?'

The Pole, looking at Bauer, quickly said a few words before his gaze swung back to the storeroom. And then he spoke, in the universal language of malice, his head nodding maliciously too.

The Jew stared at him for a few more seconds, before lowering his eyes. And then, with his elbows on his knees, his chin in his hands, his back bent, he seemed to completely ignore all of us. He was looking at a point in the storeroom that we couldn't see. But that did not dry up the flood of the Pole's words.

'Do you know him?' Bauer asked impatiently.

The Pole went silent and turned to Bauer, who pointed at the Jew with one hand, then at the Pole with the other, and then, bringing his two index fingers together, asked, 'So, do you know him?'

The Pole shook his head. He looked stunned by the question.

'So shut your mouth a bit,' said Bauer. 'Leave him in peace, and us too.'

The Pole began to speak to the three of us.

'No, shut your mouth,' Bauer said nastily, 'or we'll chuck you outside, and I'll beat the shit out of you.'

The Pole kept silent. He glanced once more at the storeroom, then went back close to the stove. He did not peel back his lips any more. His face returned to the serious, distinguished expression it had worn before, but it no longer had the same effect. It no longer meant the same thing.

I still had the flask in my hand. I leaned across to hand it back to him. But, without resentment, he signalled that I could keep hold of it. I put it on the table in front of me.

The dog had woken up and raised its head when Bauer spoke, and I noticed that the little balls of snow had begun to melt. They were no longer as round as before. There was a small puddle of water between its paws.

Bauer had seen it too. I could sense his astonishment, next to me.

'Oh, Emmerich!' he gasped.

'What?'

'Does it hurt?'

'Does what hurt?' demanded Emmerich, at first failing to grasp, as before, the joke about his balls.

Crossing his arms high around his chest, so his sides wouldn't split, Bauer pressed his mouth into his sleeve. His stifled laughter shook his body so strongly that the bench began to shake too. We could feel his laughter beneath us now.

Emmerich, sitting on the other side of Bauer, leaned forward so he could see me and silently ask me what was going on. I didn't feel that it was up to me to tell him, so I pretended not to know.

'What?' he shouted at Bauer.

But Bauer could no longer speak.

Wood burns faster than coal, so it is deceptive when you cook with it. The stove was hot, and we felt warm now — on our faces and chests, at least, because our backs were still shivering. But, at this rate, the soup would not be cooked.

Behind the mica window, the flames had died down again. And, distracted by the Pole and by everything that had happened, we hadn't noticed. What we'd drunk on our empty stomachs had put us in a good mood, and we'd forgotten about the soup needing to cook. I got up. It was the shelf's turn now. After that, it would be the table or the bench — we'd see.

It gave way easily. I hit it twice on the side with my shoulder, and it fell from the wall. It wasn't very heavy, though, so it wouldn't last long. Soon we would have to choose between the table and the bench. Or maybe we'd have to burn both, and swallow our remorse.

While I smashed the shelf into bits, Bauer suddenly thundered: 'Has he got any uncles?'

To begin with, Emmerich and I had no idea what he was talking about. I even thought for a moment that he might be referring to the Pole, and that what he had said made no sense. Emmerich was quicker to catch on than I was. He replied to Bauer: 'No, he hasn't. I wish he had right now. It would be a big help.'

He went silent, and nodded as if deep in thought.

'I think about that sometimes.'

Then he looked at Bauer. 'Why?'

'Listen,' said Bauer, pointing at me to indicate that he was talking about me as well as himself, 'tell him you're going to come home with two uncles.'

Emmerich was startled. Bauer went on: 'From this day on, we are his uncles.'

'Hang on a minute,' I said.

I was pretending, of course. I had finished breaking up the shelf and half of it had gone into the stove. I blew and blew on the wood until the flames rose up again, then I turned towards the bench. Emmerich lowered his head. Bauer, I could see, was pleased with himself for having come up with this idea. We could thank the potato alcohol for that.

'So what do you think?' he asked me.

I pretended to think a bit longer, then said, 'All right.'

Bauer clapped his hands and leaned towards Emmerich. 'Write to him that he now has two uncles. And not just any uncles.'

Then he patted Emmerich's thigh. Emmerich was so moved that he lit a cigarette. He passed one to each of us.

'But wait,' Bauer said, lifting his in the air. 'Tell him it's only on the condition that he doesn't touch a cigarette.'

'Yes,' Emmerich replied.

'Don't forget to tell him that.'

'Yes.'

Emmerich was unable to say any more than that.

But Bauer could: 'There you go! And when you write to him in future, we can write him a few words too. When we get back home, we can see him and give him a bit of money.'

Emmerich shivered and rubbed his head.

'Give it to me now,' he said, to play down his emotion.

I was still standing in front of the stove. I could hear the flames. They made little hot spots in my back. Why should I go and sit down again? A warm hand was stroking my back, up and down, and the cigarette that Emmerich had given me tasted good. I looked at him. He had kept his hand on his head. He was smiling, but had he dared, he might have sobbed.

The Pole had not looked away from us during all this time, I'd noticed. His gaze moved from one to the next as we spoke, probably searching for a word he knew. But while he might have grasped the odd phrase, he would never understand what we were talking about or what we had just decided, still less the fact that it had been partly triggered by his potato alcohol.

He asked us, using gestures, if he could smoke.

'Fuck off and die,' said Bauer.

But Emmerich offered him a cigarette. Bauer's suggestion had moved him, making him generous and goodhearted. He was already like that by nature, but now his benevolence had increased a notch.

In fact, we were all quite moved, even Bauer, because it now felt like the three of us were family. I mean, with Bauer and me becoming uncles to Emmerich's son. We'd almost forgotten how hungry we were. I looked at the window. In places, the frost was melting. Drops of water were forming and sliding down the glass. It would have been even warmer — the frost on the window would have melted even faster — had we not broken off the trapdoor, since some of the heat was disappearing up there into the attic.

We didn't forget our hunger for very long. I took out my spoon and stirred the soup. The lard had melted, and the pieces of onion were coming apart. The salami was fine too, but the cornmeal was still floating. We didn't want a broth, but a thick soup, and I was now afraid that this would end up being like something in a dream. As in a dream, we could see it, so close to us, but no matter how far we moved towards it, I had the impression we would never reach it.

The bits of shelf I'd put in had already burned up. It was going faster than I'd expected. I shoved the rest in before the flames died down completely.

'That wood must be made of paper,' I said. 'There's nothing left now. What shall we do? The bench or the table? We need to decide.'

They got up, and Bauer touched the table appraisingly.

'It's thick,' he said. 'We'd need a saw.'

Emmerich lifted up the bench. 'This too. We won't manage otherwise.'

'With three of us, we'll manage,' I said.

But no matter how hard we threw it on the floor, or from what height, it didn't break. I thought about the fence outside for a moment, but then I gave up the idea. Why go back outside and freeze my blood to wrestle with a fence that wouldn't move anyway?

So, we would be eating broth. Hot, of course, but not very filling. Leaning on the stove, smoking Emmerich's cigarette, the Pole watched us impassively. His dog was asleep. The snow sleighbells on its neck had disappeared.

'What about the door to the storeroom?' Emmerich said suddenly. 'What use is that?'

'He's right!' Bauer shouted.

Emmerich and I shoved it wide open. Seeing us coming, the Jew sat up and moved away from us, against the back wall. He watched us while we took the door off its hinges. It was heavy, but it looked easier to break than the table or the bench. We leaned it with its top propped on the bench.

'Go ahead,' I told Emmerich. 'I'll hold you.'

I took hold of his coat. He bent his knees, jumped up and landed on the door. It did not move. Not a crack appeared.

'You need to jump from higher up,' I told him.

He climbed up on the bench. Bauer and I each got hold of one of his shoulders. He jumped, and this time we heard something.

'Keep going!' we shouted, practically at the same time.

He did it again, I don't know how many times. He jumped, picking up momentum by jumping upwards from the bench. Each time, we heard the door crack a bit more. Fissures appeared. He was putting so much effort into it, you could tell, as much for us as for himself. We held him tightly, each by a shoulder. Finally, he went through it. We'd been afraid he would injure himself, that a big splinter would pierce his boots. Luckily, although he was winded, he ended up standing and unhurt, in the middle of the broken door. We gleefully smashed it into smaller pieces because there was now no doubt: with all this wood, the soup would be thick and we would eat it sitting on the bench. What a door it was! We had enough wood to fill the stove five times over.

How well the fire burned after that! The smell of it was in our nostrils, the sound of it in our ears. It gave us light too, as the sun was going down outside. Steam rose from the soup. It would be thick and nourishing — we were sure of it now. Among all the different smells, the onion was the strongest. We each drank a mouthful. It burned our tongues, but transported us to a gentler world. So we drank another. The Pole had put one elbow on the bar of the stove and was resting his temple on his hand, as easy in his mind as we were now that he knew he would be getting some soup. I no longer thought about the flash of malice I'd seen on his face. His dog sniffed occasionally.

Suddenly I realised that, without the door that we had taken down and which was now cheerfully burning, the house had changed. Was it the storeroom that had entered our space, here around the bench? Or was it the other way round? Either way, it felt very different now.

While I looked around, attempting to pinpoint the cause of this change, the Jew in the storeroom began to unbutton his coat. And then, after a moment's hesitation, he took it off, rolled it up, put it on the floor and sat on it. Because, of course, even if it was warm now in the storeroom, the floor was still freezing. It would have taken a day and a night with good coal in the stove to warm up the concrete slab.

He still wore a heavy reefer jacket under his coat, orange and dirty but very thick, and quilted, which was unusual. There were undoubtedly other layers beneath that. But it was his reefer jacket that had saved him in the forest. He had pushed his wool hat even further up his forehead. It was folded now, and from here the embroidered snowflake was invisible.

We no longer stirred on the bench, we no longer spoke. Not a single movement or sound. Each of us had been isolated from the others by the heat, the smell of the soup and the potato alcohol, and sleep was calling to us. Even the Pole was beginning to fall asleep, while leaning against the stove.

I closed my eyes for a few seconds. My imagination began to see things that weren't there. Better open them, I thought. The Pole's dog had woken up. It was still lying with its head on its front paws, and it was observing Emmerich, Bauer and me, and its kindly blinking eyes reminded me of a dog I'd once had, a long time ago.

In order to think about something else, I whispered, 'I hope he has a spoon.'

'What?' Emmerich asked, also in a whisper.

'The Pole,' I said. 'What's he going to eat with?'

'If he hasn't got one, we'll chuck him outside,' replied Bauer. 'I don't want that ugly mouth of his touching the soup.'

'Me neither,' I said.

We looked at him. He was almost asleep, leaning on the stove. Up to this point, we had been able to stand him. But soon his disgusting mouth would be eating at the table with us.

Emmerich leaned towards me with a questioning expression.

'We'll see,' I replied. 'Maybe he does have one.'

But suddenly Bauer said, 'No, we won't see. I'm going to chuck him outside, even if he does have a spoon.'

'I'll give him mine if he doesn't have one,' I joked.

But Bauer was on the warpath now. 'I want to chuck him outside. Are we scared of him?'

'Hang on, let's wait and see,' I said, putting a hand on his leg.

He calmed down a little, but not for long.

'I don't care what he does, but that mouth is not going near our soup,' he said.

All of this had been said in a whisper. The Pole was still dozing, his eyes half-closed. Suddenly Bauer yelled: 'Hey, you! What are you planning to eat with? Not with your filthy gob, I'm telling you that now. Because it makes me want to puke.'

The Pole had jumped at this. Now he was looking at each of us in turn, trying to work out who had spoken.

In a nasty voice, Bauer repeated, 'Hey, what are you planning to eat with?'

The Pole replied in his own language. We didn't know what he said, but it sounded nasty too.

We weren't afraid of him, of course, but he wasn't afraid of us either. He replied to us the way we'd spoken to him. Bauer took his spoon from a pocket and showed it to the Pole. Moving it around, he said, 'Show me yours!'

The Pole's gaze moved from the spoon to the soup to us. He was trying to understand. To help him out, Bauer pointed at him then moved the spoon closer towards him. This time, the Pole shook his head and patted his quilted jacket to say that no, he didn't have one.

'Well then, little man, you'd better go

home,' said Bauer, 'because we don't want you touching our soup. You make me sick.'

The Pole, I am sure, did not catch a single word of this, yet he understood anyway. He had sensed a threat in Bauer's voice and eyes. He began to twitch. Then he replied to Bauer, unleashing a sort of bitter, fearful litany. We did not catch a single word of it, yet we understood it anyway.

'Yeah, yeah, go ahead and cry, little man,' Bauer said.

The Pole continued to whine. Bauer nodded sympathetically and smiled sadly at him. Then suddenly the Pole moved away from the stove and crouched down in front of the remains of the storeroom door. He started searching through the bits of wood, his litany unabated. But when he found what he was looking for, he stopped talking, showed it to us, then returned to the side of the stove. He took a hideous little knife from his pocket and began feverishly sculpting his bit of wood, glancing up at us fiercely from time to time. His lips peeled back from his gums occasionally too, and his vile mouth was more terrifying to us than any evil stare.

We lit a cigarette, our last before the soup. We smoked it while watching the Pole carve his piece of wood. He had forgotten us. Concentrated, careful, he carved away, and as the daylight had continued to fade and the flames in the stove did not directly illuminate him, he moved his eyes very close to the wood. Some shavings fell on his dog. Others fell on the cast-iron stovetop and burned up instantly.

Although it was still afternoon, it looked dark enough outside to be evening. The layer of clouds between us and the sun must have grown even thicker.

The shape of the spoon appeared fairly quickly. Within a few minutes, the handle and the oval end could both be easily made out.

But what we were waiting to see was how he would make the hollow. Because without a hollow, there was no spoon. He finished the shape, looked at it for a moment, then wedged it against the stove and began to scratch at it with the point of his knife. But the wood was hard, and he seemed unable to hollow it out just by scratching. He grumbled, and looked up at us blankly, as if by staring through us he were searching for a solution. He did not look frightened by the thought of not eating if he couldn't do it, nor angry with us, just focused on his search for inspiration. And then he began working again, in a different way. We leaned forward. In the dying light, it took us a while to understand.

Still using the point of the knife, he was now tracing and retracing grooves in the wood, several times over. When two grooves became deep enough, he broke off the wood between them. And so on.

'He's going to do it,' I said.

'In that case, he's going to pay for his soup,' said Bauer, turning round to take the flask from the table.

But before taking a drink, he hesitated. He turned the flask in his hands, looked down at his boots, lifted his head, and said, 'Or we could just chuck him outside. Spoon or no spoon, he still makes me want to puke.'

'Make him pay,' I said, to calm Bauer down.

'Yeah, that's better,' Emmerich agreed.

Emmerich and I were not afraid of the Pole. But being here felt like returning to a childhood home, and we didn't want to spoil the innocent mood. We were smoking cigarettes, warm and cosy in front of the flames that lit up our faces with a familiar light, our senses floating gently in the smell of the soup. If we threw the Pole outside, that would mean fighting, getting riled up, opening the door and letting in the cold, and almost certainly fighting again once we were outside. We feared that, after all of that, we would end up eating the soup in full awareness of the discomfort of this filthy little Polish hovel, our emotions still riled up, and that the soup would stick in our throats.

Bauer took a good swig and handed me the flask. I took a good swig too. Emmerich didn't want any more. Bauer stood up and put more wood in the stove. And while he was stirring the soup with his spoon, the Pole, without looking up, still carving his wood, muttered something, and Bauer replied: 'Keep working, little man, instead of talking. Hurry up — it's nearly cooked.'

'Is that true?' I asked.

'Yeah, the cornmeal's getting thicker. It's sticking to the bottom.'

'So unstick it,' I said. 'It'll burn.'

He did that, then asked me to hand him the flask. And the amount of alcohol he poured into the soup! It was partly to make the Pole pay, and partly because we would be eating it so soon, the taste of the alcohol would not have time to evaporate.

Bauer handed me the almost empty flask, and the Pole finished working with his knife. He put it away in his pocket and began sanding the spoon's hollow on a corner of the stove. He showed no fear: he pressed down with all his strength, as though he were sanding a tree stump.

'If he breaks it now,' said Bauer, closing his eyes to imagine this happening, 'I will die laughing.'

'Let me see,' I said to the Pole, gesturing with my hand.

He stopped sanding and stared at me. I made the same gesture, more insistently, and he handed me the spoon with a threatening look on his face. I turned it in my hands, examining the hollow, weighing it up, and said (because it was the truth): 'It's pretty well done.'

I passed it to Emmerich. 'Yeah,' he agreed. 'He's done it.'

'Give it to me,' said Bauer, holding out his hand.

'What are you going to do?'

'Throw it in the fire.'

The Pole stared at Emmerich. Bauer was still holding out his hand, grinning now, his eyes fierce. Emmerich figured out the best way to do it. He moved the spoon close to

Bauer — but careful not to get too close — and turned it around so that he could see it from every angle. Then he handed it back to the Pole. Still grinning, Bauer said, 'It's ready.'

He grabbed the saucepan's handle with two hands and placed it carefully on the table, then he went back to the stove and picked up the slices of bread. Emmerich and I turned around so we were facing the table, and took out our spoons and tin mugs. Bauer stepped over the bench and sat between us.

And suddenly the hunger, which had left us for a while — that hunger sent to sleep by the cigarettes and the potato alcohol and the fire in the stove — awoke and rose from the saucepan and fell upon us as if it were a living creature. The soup looked good and smelled good. The slices of salami floated on the surface, carried there by the cornmeal, now cooked. The melted lard was still boiling.

We turned away from the stove, and the heat caressed our backs. We watched steam rise from the soup. My head was spinning. We looked at the slices of bread. The soup was continuing to simmer. The edges of the bread were toasted, reminding us of things past. As if imparting a secret, but loud enough for Emmerich to hear too, Bauer said to me: 'We'll tell our nephew about this.'

Relaxed and fully in agreement, I nodded. Emmerich whispered, 'We mustn't forget.'

I leaned across so he could see me, and pointed to my forehead. 'It's in here,' I told him. 'We won't forget anything.'

Emmerich scratched his head and gave me a smile like nothing I've ever seen: happy, sad, grateful . . . a smile to make you weep. On the table, our shadows danced.

The Pole appeared next to Emmerich, spoon in hand. If we had moved up, he could have sat down at the end of the bench, next to Emmerich or to me. But we didn't think about that, and neither did he. The question never arose. I noticed that his hands were less ravaged by the cold than ours were. He blew on his spoon.

'And the plate,' Bauer said, drawing a circle with his hands. 'You forgot to make one. Tough luck.'

The Pole understood and looked afraid. I was afraid too — afraid that we'd have to beat him up and get angry if it turned nasty, just at the moment when we were sitting at the table, starving once more. Only, Bauer was right. What was he going to eat from? We hadn't thought of that. We hadn't imagined him eating out of the saucepan.

'Hurry up,' said Bauer. 'Go and make one now before it gets cold.'

He half-laughed, nastily. The Pole, suddenly very pale, gripped his spoon in one hand as if he were going to break it and opened his mouth to speak.

'Shut your face,' Bauer told him, and pushed his own mug in front of him. There was no fraternity or kindness in the gesture, of course, just the desire, shared by all of us, to finally eat.

The Pole, still very pale, stared at Bauer, his eyes rolling. In his head, everything was upside down and going too fast.

Bauer served us in our mugs and drew the saucepan towards him. And then we began to eat. We bit into the hot bread. We smelled the flavour and thickness of the soup. All of it was good: the bread, the Italians' cornmeal, the slices of melting salami. We could smell the alcohol too.

We burned our tongues and palates. We were happy, but not for long, because the Pole suddenly stopped eating in that strange way he had — like an old woman, with his missing teeth — and his eyes turned to slits as his mouth was deformed by a fierce grin. We stopped eating too, and watched him.

From where he stood, he was facing the storeroom. The Jew was dozing, sitting on his coat. The Pole spoke a few words, not very loud, but we understood that they were addressed to the Jew, and that they were filled with satisfaction and contempt. It was a strange kind of curse.

'Don't start that again,' Bauer told him.

The Pole shut up, but lifted his steaming mug towards the storeroom as his face split once again into that vile grin. It was probably that smile that caused Bauer to decide on something that Emmerich and I had never considered — because we were not Bauer, and also, I guess, because we'd drunk a lot less potato alcohol than he had.

So he looked scornfully at the Pole for a moment and then, without saying anything, turned towards the storeroom. 'Come over here,' he called.

The Jew lifted his head and looked over at us.

'Get up, come over here,' said Bauer, indicating the free side of the table, facing the Pole.

'What are you doing? What for?' I asked, although I had understood.

Bauer shot me a look. Then, ignoring me, he touched the saucepan handle and called out in a loud voice: 'Come and eat. Go on, get up and come over here.'

'No,' I said. 'Stop. Leave him where he is.'

'Why?' Bauer asked, as the Jew slowly, hesitantly stood up.

Once he was on his feet, he bent down to pick up his coat, but Bauer signalled that he should leave it there. Then he made another hand gesture to say he should come out of the storeroom.

'No, Bauer,' I repeated. 'Leave him where he is.'

Again, Bauer asked, 'Why?'

I didn't reply. What was the point? He knew the answer. He knew the risk we were taking with our morale by inviting him to eat with us.

In early autumn, two Jews — two brothers, we thought — used to do our laundry. They soaped it, put it in hot water in a bathtub outside, and then hung it out to dry. Sometimes we walked past them. Sometimes we watched them work. One day, after watching them for a while, we'd talked to them about the way they rinsed the clothes. We thought it wasn't good. It seemed to us that we could still see the soap in the hanging clothes. It was almost enough to make us itch. They tried to understand what we wanted, though I'm not sure they succeeded. But, as they'd made the effort, we slipped each of them a cigarette. And after that, they folded our clothes first, even our underwear, and brought them to our beds in the gymnasium. If we were there when they did that, we would slip them each another cigarette. And instead of smoking a whole one each, they cut them in two so they could have two smokes during the day.

Except that, when their turn came, we remembered them. For the whole of October, it had been their hands that washed and folded our laundry, and our cigarettes that they smoked. And, unfortunately for them, and for us, among the hundred or so soldiers who were there that day, it was in front of Bauer and me that they lay down, on their stomachs, in the clearing. Bauer and I wanted to change places with other soldiers, but as we hesitated, wondering how to do it, the others next to us had already fired. So we had no choice: we shot our laundrymen. And just before we pulled the trigger, one of them had thrown us a look full of sadness — because he was going to die, of course, but also, so it seemed to us, because we were the ones who were killing him.

Bauer and I felt depressed that day. More than usual, I mean. And it was a different, particular kind of depression. In the evening, we talked about it, outside. The weather was good. Emmerich helped us. We understood that the solution was simple: with the new laundrymen, we would not look at them or talk to them. We wouldn't do anything with them that had anything to do with life.

Bauer had asked me why the Jew should stay in the storeroom. But he knew the answer, you see. He'd known it since October.

The Jew was now almost out of the storeroom. He took another step forward and stopped in the doorway. He waited there as if on the threshold of a house. Bauer signalled to him to keep going. So he came out of the storeroom and moved towards the table. A vein was throbbing on his temple. The side of his mouth was quivering. He didn't know what to do with his hands. He put them behind his back, then brought them back in front and crossed them. His gaze never wavered. And yet he managed not to look at anyone. He stared at a point on the wall, close to the window. Just beneath his hat, his vein was still throbbing.

The Pole, standing up in front of him, starting drumming his spoon nervously on the table. Rage was shining in his eyes.

'Shut your face,' Bauer told him. 'Eat. Get stuck in. It'll choke you later, you'll see.'

The Pole stopped drumming, put his hands on the table, leaned towards Bauer, and spoke to him in a voice full of suppressed rage, drawing back his lips, not like a dead fish any more, but like an animal. And he leaned ever closer to Bauer, looking as if he wanted to rip his heart out. He was so enraged with Bauer that I looked over at our rifles. Bauer didn't seem bothered, though. He listened seriously, attentively, as though the Pole was confiding in him.

Suddenly the Pole stood up and looked

away from Bauer, his rage replaced by laughter as he pointed his spoon at the Jew, who was still staring towards the window. There was not even a shadow of good cheer in that laugh. I noticed his dog, which had been lying next to the stove, now sat up.

Then, as the Pole gradually stopped laughing, I leaned towards Bauer and Emmerich. 'Let's chuck him outside. I've had enough of this.'

'Me too,' said Emmerich. 'I'm hungry.'

'No,' Bauer said happily, 'he's going to pay for his soup. He's going to eat with a Jew. He'll remember that.'

But I really had had enough of all this, and of Bauer too, a little. So I pointed at the Jew and said coldly, 'We're going to pay for it too. We won't be able to kill him after this.'

What I meant was that, if we had to do it, it would be hard. Bauer asked me, 'Why?'

'Remember the autumn?' I said. 'How depressed we got over our laundrymen.'

'The autumn was a long time ago.'

And then, with a hand gesture, he erased something in the air, and said, 'Anyway, who'll do that? Not us. We're bringing one back. So tomorrow, it's certain, Graaf will let us go out again. We'll come back here.'

'Maybe,' I said, a little doubtfully. 'We'll see.'

But really, he was right. I chased away a fear: that Graaf would prevent us leaving anyway, just for the pleasure of it. So I didn't argue any more, mainly because I was hungry and I wanted to feel happy again, the way we'd felt when we started to eat, a little earlier.

Emmerich felt the same way. He pushed his mug in front of the Jew and pulled the saucepan a bit closer to him so he could share it with Bauer.

The Jew stopped looking at the point on the wall and turned his gaze to Emmerich's mug. His hands, still crossed in front of him, started to move. He pursed his lips. His face relaxed. The embroidered snowflake on his hat was half-concealed in a fold. But I could still see part of it. I wanted to eat in peace. I signalled to him to take off his hat. He took it off and put it in his pocket, and now, without his hat, with his hair falling around his face, we could see even more clearly how young he was.

We didn't hear any more from the Pole. Hunger had swallowed up his laughter. He waited, spoon in hand, motionless apart from his eyes. His dog was lying down again next to the stove. It was licking the puddle of water made by the snow sleighbells when they melted.

Bauer gave the signal. He took a slice of salami from the saucepan and accompanied it with a mouthful of toasted bread. Everyone else followed suit.

Thus began the strangest meal we ever had in Poland.

Outside, through the window, the light was dim and still fading. The flames in the stove lit us up from behind. As we ate, our shadows accompanied us by dancing on the table.

So, one last time, this is where each of us was, how we were eating, and what we were eating with. Emmerich, Bauer and I were sitting on the bench, in that order. Emmerich and Bauer were both eating from the saucepan, and I was eating from my mug. The Pole, standing next to Emmerich, was eating from Bauer's mug with the spoon he'd carved from the storeroom door. Facing him, standing next to me, the Jew was eating from Emmerich's mug, without a spoon.

The soup was tasty, hot and filling. The bread was still warm. We made noises as we ate. The fire, behind us, added its own sounds. What a beautiful music, or silence, that was: the sounds of the food in our mouths and the fire in the stove.

All of it — onions, salami, cornmeal — melted in the mouth. We were happy again. Occasionally, without meaning to, I caught the Jew's eye. What I read in his eyes had no meaning at all. I mean to say that, the way he looked at me, he seemed to be saying that all of this — what we were eating, the fire in the stove, the evening light coming through the window — had, for him, no meaning at all. But he ate. He picked up the cornmeal with his fingers, then licked his fingers and drank the soup in small mouthfuls. The melted lard left traces of white around his lips.

Several times, I saw Emmerich lift his head from the saucepan he was sharing with Bauer and look up at the ceiling. Then he looked at the Jew, and went back to the saucepan. Bauer and he ate politely, each waiting for the other to take a spoonful of soup before putting their own spoon in.

Behind us, the Pole's dog had fallen back to sleep, and now and then it made little whimpers.

As we ate, and the soup disappeared, the music changed. The spoons made more noise in the mugs and the saucepan. Suddenly, out of nowhere, Emmerich murmured, 'We should let him go.'

'What?' Bauer asked. 'Who are you talking about?'

'Him,' Emmerich replied, pointing to the Jew with his spoon, without looking at him.

'What are you on about?' Bauer asked. 'Why?'

But Emmerich said nothing. For a moment, we waited.

'Come on, why?' Bauer insisted.

'I don't know. Because.'

'You should eat,' Bauer said in a quiet, kind voice.

Emmerich started eating again.

I finished my bread. I glanced at Emmerich. I didn't know what he'd meant, really. I fished the last slice of salami from the soup, and before eating it I said to Bauer, 'This is the best meal we've ever had.'

'Yeah.'

He pointed to the Pole's flask. 'That's good stuff. It tastes bad when you drink it, but for cooking . . . we should have it every day.'

'We should tell Kropp,' I joked.

I had just swallowed the salami when Emmerich, in the same murmur he'd used before, said, 'It'd make us feel better, don't you think?'

For a moment, I thought he was talking about Kropp, the cook. I had no idea what was supposed to make us feel better. But Bauer, quicker than me, asked him: 'What are you talking about, Emmerich? What would make us feel better?'

His spoon hanging in mid-air, Emmerich turned towards the Jew and said, 'Letting him go.'

'What for?' Bauer asked.

'In the future, when we thought about him, we'd feel better.'

'I don't see why,' said Bauer.

The Pole, hearing us, sat up straight and watched us tensely.

'You,' Bauer told him, 'look away and eat.'

To Emmerich, he asked: 'What would have been the point of us freezing our balls off?'

'We'd have been freezing anyway.'

'But we were out in it all day. And now you want to let him crawl back into his hole?'

Emmerich looked down at the saucepan. After a moment, he started eating again.

But Bauer wouldn't let it go. 'Come on. What for?'

Emmerich sighed, but almost imperceptibly, like a cow in a distant field. The Jew, having drunk all his soup, held the mug close to his lips and used two fingers to scrape the last bits of cornmeal into his mouth. Then, when he noticed me watching him, he looked embarrassed and stopped what he was doing. But he had no spoon, so it was fine for him to eat like that. I signalled that he should continue. Bauer, sitting with his shoulder against mine, shot me a look, referring to what Emmerich had begun saying. Then he stood up, and I heard him putting more wood in the stove.

From the corner of his eye, Emmerich watched the Jew, who had begun eating with his fingers again.

'Great idea to use that door,' said Bauer, returning to the bench. 'It's as good as coal.'

'Yeah,' I said. 'It saved us.'

He took a big spoonful of cornmeal from the saucepan. Swallowing it, he sighed with satisfaction. It really was cooked to perfection, and it tasted good too. The salami was the dominant flavour. To begin with, we'd felt like we were losing it by putting it in the soup. But not any more. It was true, I thought: we should tell Kropp about our recipe.

Everyone was finishing their cornmeal now. We were scraping the sides and the bottom. Soon, it was all gone.

The Pole finished his soup in a hurry, perhaps because he thought that Bauer might take the mug off him, or perhaps because the hunger was gnawing at him more and more. His spoon went straight from the mug to his mouth, never stopping for a second, although all it held each time was a few bits of cornmeal.

Bauer and I finished eating, both of us thinking of what Emmerich had said about the Jew. It was circling around in our heads and our bellies now. We were still hungry, but we'd lost a bit of the happiness we'd felt at the beginning.

Emmerich pushed the saucepan slowly

towards Bauer, to let him know he could finish it on his own.

'You sure?' Bauer asked.

Emmerich nodded.

'There's still a bit left,' Bauer said.

'I know,' said Emmerich. 'But I'm fine.'

While Emmerich took out a cigarette to mark the official end of his meal, Bauer stared into the saucepan as if he were reading something, and said, 'Why should he go back to his hole? We went to so much trouble. We left without eating breakfast. We froze our balls off. What was the point of it all?'

Emmerich took his time lighting the cigarette. Then he leaned across so he could see us both, Bauer and me.

'The point is, at least we'd have done it once.'

He took a drag on his cigarette. He drummed on the table. He fidgeted like crazy. And then he turned as still as a statue.

'How many have we killed?' he asked, trying to control his voice. 'It's making us sick. We've had it up to here. We should let him go. When we think about him, we'll feel better.'

He looked straight ahead, and then at the ceiling, and said, 'When we dream at night, we'll dream about him.'

'Personally,' said Bauer, 'I'll feel sick

tomorrow if Graaf makes us stay there because we didn't bring any back. I'm feeling sick now, just thinking about it.'

'Me too,' said Emmerich. 'But if we look beyond tomorrow, we'll be able to remember that at least we've done it once.'

'I can't look beyond tomorrow,' Bauer said.

He began scraping the cornmeal from the sides of the saucepan. I had almost finished mine. It had gone cold and made a crust at the bottom of the mug. Bauer noticed this, and lifted the saucepan to give me some more because he had more left than I did. I lifted my hand to say no, thank you.

'How far can you look?' he asked me. 'Tomorrow? The day after tomorrow?'

Emmerich was leaning over and watching me, awaiting my response. I shook my head slowly, not knowing what to say, not knowing who was right. As I didn't reply, Emmerich said to me in a gentle, sad voice, 'You were lucky to go on your tram last night. For me, the nights are as bad as the days. Sometimes they're worse.'

I tried to smile at him, then lowered my eyes.

You see? I was right. We should keep our dreams to ourselves. We should never talk about them. There had not been even the shadow of a reproach in Emmerich's voice, but I still felt bad that I was luckier than him.

'I'm not always on a tram,' I said, trying to keep my voice light. 'That was the first time.'

'I've never been on one,' Emmerich murmured.

Though Bauer was silent, I could see he was frowning, closing in on himself. He pushed the saucepan away, and I saw that there was still some cornmeal left at the bottom and on the sides. The Pole saw this too, and leaned down. He said something, with a scowl, and Bauer shot him a look full of hatred. The Pole mirrored his expression. But he didn't touch the saucepan.

Some time passed. Now that my hunger was gone, tiredness took its place. I half-closed my eyes. I wanted to go home. But home was too far away. I would have needed more time, and more imagination. So I stayed there, next to Emmerich and Bauer, in that little Polish house that had scared us when we first found it.

Night had fallen behind the only window. Had it not been for the fire in the stove, we would have been sitting in the dark. And I felt, more intensely than I usually did, that wherever we were — Emmerich, Bauer and I — that was home. It was warm, and the firelight was pleasant. So it was a shame, I thought a little bitterly, that Emmerich had chosen this particular moment to torture himself.

Now he had finished eating, the Jew seemed unsure whether to go back to the storeroom or remain standing next to the table. I wasn't sure what he should do either. He licked his lips where the melted lard had left traces of white.

The Pole sniffed loudly, looked around, and went suddenly towards the stove. We heard him moving around, and when he reappeared at the table, he was wearing his fur hood again, his scarf wound tight around his neck and his coat buttoned up. He took his large green flask and put it back in his pocket. Picking up his wooden spoon, he put it in the mug Bauer had lent him and pushed it towards him, smiling exaggeratedly at him with his toothless mouth.

Then he said something to us in his language, before walking towards the door and calling his dog. 'Fuck off and die yourself,' Bauer replied. 'And hurry up, about it.'

The door banged shut. The icy air swept over us for a moment, and we shivered. Then the warmth of the fire returned, and we felt at home once again. But we had remembered how it felt to be cold.

Grabbing hold of his mug, Bauer thrust it

up in the air quickly as though he was going to throw it away. But the mug stayed in his hand. It was the Pole's wooden spoon that flew over the table and landed on the other side of the room. The Jew watched this, then turned back towards us, and for a moment it looked as if he was about to smile. We saw a glimmer in his eyes, which relaxed his face. The rings around his young eyes disappeared a little bit. Emmerich looked at him for what seemed like forever.

Bauer, still holding his mug, breathed deeply, the way he does sometimes when he's asleep. I saw his chest rise and fall. I listened to his breathing and the wood burning in the stove. I heard it all as though it was coming from my own chest.

'Tomorrow morning,' Bauer said suddenly, 'Graaf will hit the iron outside. And if we haven't taken him back with us, we won't be able to get out of it. If there are any left to kill, we'll have to kill them.'

He let go of the mug and pushed it away. Crossing his hands behind the back of his neck, he asked without looking at anyone, 'Yes or no?'

We didn't reply. He turned towards me.

'Yes,' I said.

Then, without looking at Emmerich, he said, 'Yes or no?'

Like me, Emmerich could only respond with the simple truth: that, if we we went back empty-handed, Graaf, our lieutenant, would refuse to let us leave the following day, and we would be obliged to take part in the shootings.

'Yes,' he said.

Bauer removed his hands from the back of his neck and put them in the air in front of him, to say that we all thought the same thing, so what was the point in talking about it any longer. But Emmerich's *yes* floated, fragile and uncertain, and he whispered, 'I'm telling you, Bauer. One day, I will have need of him. I would rather kill some tomorrow if it means I'll be able to remember this one when I need to. Even now, tonight, it'll make me feel better.'

He stopped talking, though not for long. Without looking at us, he added: 'You too, you'll have need of him.'

Bauer took his time lighting a cigarette, then replied: 'No, not me. One wouldn't be enough.'

He blew out smoke and muttered to himself, 'Just one!'

He smoked a bit more, and then, as if casually, he said, 'You were the one who found him, Emmerich.'

'What difference does that make?' Emmerich

asked, earnestly. 'Why?'

In a resigned voice, innocent of any malice, Bauer replied: 'It's no use finding him and then crying about it afterwards.'

'No, no, no,' Emmerich started, endlessly it seemed, because he didn't add anything, and neither did we. And the Jew, probably disturbed by this silence, and with nothing left to keep him there, went back to sit in the storeroom. He moved silently, as light as a bird.

It was the fire dying in the stove that pulled us out of that silence. The cold knocked two or three times at our backs, as if it were knocking on a door. We shivered, and moved about on the bench, remembering that we had to go.

And then Bauer said what I knew he would say, the words I'd been waiting for and dreading. He turned slightly towards me, hesitated for a moment, and finally asked me what I thought we should do with the Jew. Now I had the casting vote, given that he and Emmerich couldn't agree.

As if I were still hesitating, I said, 'Hang on.'

I leaned over so I could see Emmerich. He was staring at the table, motionless. He turned towards me, blinked, and stared back down at the table again.

Unfortunately for me, I remembered, just then, the interminable look he had given the Jew a bit earlier. I understood that look now. I knew who Emmerich had seen, secretly, when he looked through the Jew, and who, in his imagination, we would be taking back or letting go. And now, this very evening, I had the power to make him feel better. I could help him out. I could understand, better than ever, his love and concern for his son, and I could help him to worry a bit less about him. But I'd had enough, and thinking of tomorrow — imagining Graaf preventing us leaving — was making me feel sick. And even if Emmerich hadn't lied to us, if it really had been the Jew he wanted to save, Bauer was right anyway. My God, how could he think that one Jew would be enough to make us feel better when we dreamed of him at night?

So I gave my opinion of what to do with the Jew, knowing that I was going to break Emmerich's soul, but hoping that it wouldn't be broken for long. Just for this evening. For one night only. I prayed that Emmerich's broken heart and broken soul would mend quickly, and that he would forget all of this, just like all the rest.

But I wouldn't have done that, I swear, had I known what chance had in store for us, had I known what awaited Emmerich in the spring, not far from here, under the bridge in Galicia. And that the only bravery Bauer and I would show was in not looking away while he died.

It was night when we left the house. The storeroom door was all burned. In the light from the embers, we slipped back into our clothes. Outside, the cold took us by surprise. In the doorway, the Jew put on his coat, his fur mittens and his hat.

We took him back to the company, and the next day, we were allowed to leave again at dawn, before the first executions. Clouds raced past the setting moon. A cat crossed the road. In the frozen night, I wanted to remember a prayer I could say for Emmerich and his broken soul, but all that came to mind were odd words, just little remnants of prayers. We walked through a hamlet. Light glowed from behind a window. Emmerich walked ahead of us, alone. I couldn't remember a whole prayer, but I did what I could with those remnants.